Cutter Boy

Cutter Boy

Cristy Watson

James Lorimer & Company Ltd., Publishers
Toronto

Copyright © by Cristy Watson
Canadian edition published in 2016. United States edition published in 2017.

James Lorimer & Company Ltd., Publishers acknowledges the support of the Ontario Arts Council. We acknowledge the support of the Canada Council for the Arts which last year invested $24.3 million in writing and publishing throughout Canada. We acknowledge the Government of Ontario through the Ontario Media Development Corporation's Ontario Book Initiative.

ONTARIO ARTS COUNCIL
CONSEIL DES ARTS DE L'ONTARIO

The Canada Council | Le Conseil des Arts
for the Arts | du Canada

Canadä

Cover design: Tyler Cleroux
Cover image: Shutterstock

Library and Archives Canada Cataloguing in Publication

Watson, Cristy, 1964-, author
        Cutter boy / Cristy Watson.

(SideStreets)
Issued in print and electronic formats.
ISBN 978-1-4594-1098-5 (bound).--ISBN 978-1-4594-1095-4 (pbk).--
ISBN 978-1-4594-1096-1 (epub)

        I. Title. II. Series: SideStreets

PS8645.A8625C88 2016   jC813'.6   C2015-907190-9
                                                       C2015-907191-7

James Lorimer &   Canadian edition   American edition
Company Ltd., Publishers   (978-1-4594-1095-4)   (978-1-4594-1098-5)
117 Peter St., Suite 304   distributed by: distributed by:
Toronto, ON, Canada   Formac Lorimer Books   Lerner Publishing Group
M5V 2G9   5502 Atlantic Street   1251 Washington Ave N
www.lorimer.ca   Halifax, NS, Canada   Minneapolis, MN, USA
                               B3H 1G4   55401

Printed and bound in Canada.
Manufactured by Friesens Corporation in Altona, Manitoba, Canada in
May 2016.
Job #222731

This book is dedicated to all the youth who bravely face each day and each new challenge. It is also dedicated to the friends who reach out with their support, and to the teachers and counsellors who care and listen.

To Shelley and Kathleen — you are remembered well!

Prologue

The First Cut

The first time I cut is as clear as if it happened yesterday.

Everybody remembers their first time. It's like riding a bike or a roller coaster. It stays with you. The fear. The excitement. The adrenaline.

It had been a grey month of low clouds and weeks of rain. The grey seeped into everything it touched, like a black-and-white cartoon when it gets wet and the colours blur together. It was the day my twin sisters left for McGill University in Montreal.

Naomi and Dee were into neon. Pink, green, and purple were their favourites. They talked fast and laughed a lot — mostly at each other's jokes. But I felt included. I felt like I was a part of something. When they left, I guess they took the colour and laughter with them.

I remember begging them to pick Simon Fraser or UBC so they would be close by, but they wanted McGill, and that was it. While Mom and Dad drove them to the Vancouver Airport, with the car loaded with luggage, I went to my room. I passed the bathroom on my way so I could grab the razor blade.

It wasn't like I had planned this for months. It was more like my feet took me to the bathroom. My hands pulled the blade from the drawer. My sleeve was rolled up, my skin smooth and ready.

The first razor prick was hard. It was too deep so I bled like crazy. I remember running back to the bathroom and washing the blood away.

That cut wasn't calming at all. It didn't make me feel different. Or better. But there was pain. And in that moment, I realized the pain was something I could control. It wasn't as though someone was *doing* something to hurt me — I was *choosing* to cut. I was choosing to experience the moment.

My second attempt was not so deep but it pierced my skin enough that blood seeped from my arm. Red infiltrated the grey and I knew I would cut again.

And again.

And again.

Chapter 1

Invisible

Mom pushes the plate of food in my general direction. She avoids eye contact. It's a miracle the plate doesn't slide off the table. Our hands nearly brush as I reach for it, but only air passes between us. Dad doesn't notice. He's already cut a piece of steak and jammed it in his mouth. His jaw cracks as he chews and reads the paper. Mom flips open a magazine about jogging.

"Guess that means we're eating alone, as usual," I say, "but at the same table."

My parents shift in their seats, but don't say anything.

"Travis . . . how's your steak?" I ask myself out loud. Trying to be funny has no effect. They don't even crack a smile. Most fifteen-year-old guys don't want their parents nagging at them through supper. Most teens hate small talk and having to answer twenty-question grillings. But I'd welcome a question or lecture — anything to show I exist.

Through the silence, I hear the rumble of cars on the street. One of our neighbours opens a garbage can in the back alley. The clank of metal against metal makes my mom jump. Dad looks at her over the newspaper, then places his hand over hers. His gaze returns to the paper, using it as a grey wall of defence.

I grab my plate and kick my chair in as I leave the table. No one notices.

I wonder what would happen if I threw my plate against the wall, if I watched as it shattered into a thousand pieces. That's how my feelings would shatter, if I released them.

I carry my supper up the stairs to my bedroom. As I close the door, I hear my parents sigh with relief. They don't start up a conversation right away but I'm sure that in a few minutes they'll talk to each other about their day.

I slam the plate onto my desk. It vibrates and some of the juice splashes onto my homework. I smudge the page trying to clean it with my shirt sleeve, then give up and collapse beside my bed. Without thinking, I reach between the mattresses to the hole I've made. I grasp the edge of my blade. I pull it out carefully and place it beside my plate.

While I cut my steak, I hear muffled voices downstairs — talk that doesn't include me.

But I bet it's about me. And how I'm not the son they hoped for.

I roll my finger over the smooth metal of the razor. I get a rhythm going, and my breathing begins to match it. I eat at the same pace. The meat is tasteless and the food leaves me feeling empty. But when I turn the blade in my hands, it sparkles, as the light from my lamp hits it.

I get up and walk across my bedroom to make sure the door is locked. It's an old habit from when my sisters lived here. They would barge in at any time. Now they've been at McGill for three years — three years without them hogging the bathroom, or playing dance music all night long. Three years without them asking how my school day went or offering their help and advice.

I wish my sisters were here now, ranting like they used to about boys and school. I wish I could ask them about Mom and Dad, so they could help me understand why all I get is the silent treatment. But discussing our parents always upsets them.

I pull my shirt sleeve over my shoulder. I never expose my arms to anyone. Especially not during PE — that's why I don't change my shirt in front of the guys. I wouldn't want them to see my scars. So, I usually hover in the corner, hoping no one will notice me. All the other guys walk around without their shirts, flexing their biceps to show off their muscles.

Tomorrow I have to face them again. Weekends are when I try to get my head straight so I can handle the crap the guys give me all week. But I was ignored at dinner again and it's not like I have anyone to talk to.

I'm surrounded by grey. Even my school is made of concrete — like a prison.

Grey school.

Grey home.

Grey family.

But I have a secret weapon against the grey, something that keeps me alive. Just thinking about piercing my skin gets my adrenaline going. It feels like my insides light up. And every time I carve into my flesh, I feel my body settle into a calm, quiet place.

I hold the blade in my right hand and look

down at my left arm. Seventeen cuts — I know this without counting. I'm left-handed so my right arm is already full of scars. Soon I'll have to resort to my inner thighs. I press the blade against my skin. It's cold. I notice that the razor is grey, too. I slide it across my flesh and feel the sting, the prick, and then the grey disappears.

Red seeps from beneath the blade and drips down my arm. I catch it with the tissue I pull from my bedside drawer then watch as the crimson creeps into a pattern. Along my arm is a perfect line — one of my best. I've seen pictures on the Internet of people who cut. Some slice anywhere. Not me. I take pride in doing this well. A pattern of scars flows down my arms, criss-crossing everywhere.

I take a deep breath; breathe in the rush of sensation along my flesh.

I dab at the cut until it stops bleeding. I love the purity of the colour that is trapped within me until I set it free. The red proves I am alive.

Once the bleeding stops, I pull my sleeve down. I cautiously open my door. It's Sunday, so Dad's still home. Weeknights he's back out the door to his office — pulling a late-nighter. When I'm certain it's clear, I cross the hall to the bathroom and lock the door behind me. After flushing the bloodied tissue, I rinse the blade under the tap. Even the red that slides into the sink is beautiful as it swirls down the drain. Everything is calm and quiet.

It's late when I finally brush my teeth. I fill a glass with water and head back to my room.

The door clicks shut.

No one calls up to say good night.

Chapter 2

New Kid in Town

Mondays are the worst. I have two blocks of PE, back to back, and my gym class is all guys. What a set-up! Want to be bullied? Just place all the testosterone in one room.

I take my time getting changed for PE. It's basketball, and because the other guys have a game coming up they are keen to be out on the court playing, so I make it into the gym without being noticed. When I get to the bleachers, Mr. Mackie has already completed the roll call.

"Travis, I just marked you absent. Two more lates and they'll count against you." He shakes his bald head at me, then marches to the middle of the gymnasium where he blows his whistle.

I get hell for taking a few extra minutes to get dressed. But any other day, the whole class can harass me about being useless at sports without a comment from the teacher? Half the time Morgan and TJ throw me into the lockers, calling it their "warm up" for gym. Others, like Mandeep, just stand by and let it happen. And Mr. Mackie ignores what's really going on.

I'm so stressed about how I'm going to pass PE this term that I almost miss her. She's tall, and her slim body is accented with smooth muscles. Her dark skin glows with a soft sheen under the gym lights. She glances toward the exit from the gym and back to the floor, while she shifts restlessly, on her feet.

"Boys, I'd like you to meet Chyvonne Caldwell." Mr. Mackie waves her over to our group. "She will be in our class until something can be worked out with her schedule. She's taking a grade *ten* course that conflicts with the PE time for grade *nine* girls."

Several of my classmates snicker and look at her the way they usually look at me. They're probably sizing her up as a new target for their bullying. Normally, I'd be glad for the distraction, but I'm pretty sure she didn't ask to be here any more than I did.

"We're going to practise our drills. Travis, can you show Chyvonne what we're doing so she can join us?" That brings a roar of laughter from the rest of the class.

Chyvonne's chest swells as she takes a deep breath, and my body reacts as I catch myself staring. Before I can turn away, a basketball *whaps* against my head.

"Oh, *sorry!*" says Morgan, as he and TJ laugh.

Mandeep grabs them by their shirts. "Come on, dudes — let's play." They ignore

Mr. Mackie's instructions to do drills and start a game at the other end of the gym. TJ grabs the net as he drives the basketball through it.

Chyvonne taps my shoulder. I look up into her eyes. They aren't brown, to match her skin tone, but a shade of gold. They are almost yellow, like a cat's.

I want to ask if they are contacts. I find myself looking at her eyes from several angles. Just as I decide it is her true eye colour, I realize she's smiling at me. Still unsure of how to start the conversation, I smile back nervously.

Chyvonne scans the gym and says, "Since I'm the only girl in the class, I'll have to work twice as hard to show I can keep up." She picks up a ball that rolls past her feet and hurls it across the gym. She almost makes a basket!

"I think that qualifies as keeping up," I say. She laughs.

Now that Chyvonne is standing so close to me, I feel sweat pool under my armpits and a wave of excitement courses through my lower body. My brain stalls. I drop my eyes to try to regain control. Chyvonne is wearing a pair of pink Air Zoom Nikes with yellow laces. My scruffy runners are a Walmart special. Chyvonne's outfit matches — yellow shorts and a lighter yellow tank top with the number five stitched onto it. My ratty shorts and long-sleeved shirt should really be trashed. As I look up, I realize she's taller than most of the guys in the class. And her black hair, thick with wild curls, adds to her height.

Chyvonne pipes up, "Do you even like basketball?"

"Ahh . . . more to the point, do I even like *gym*? No. My mom does enough exercise for the both of us." As soon as I say it, I regret the words. *What the hell?* Like Chyvonne would care about my mom.

"Travis! I asked you to help our new student with the drills!" Mr. Mackie hollers. "I suggest you make yourself *useful*."

Again, laughter fills the gym.

"Let me show *you* some tricks," says Chyvonne. She grabs a ball from the cart and rolls it between her hands like Steve Nash. Then she glides across the gym floor and makes an easy basket.

"Wow. Are you on a team or something?"

"Yeah. Well, I was. I played back in Toronto. Here I'll have trouble making *any* team. I'm too late for tryouts. I'm a point guard, but I hear your girls' team already has three people for that position."

Point guard. We're going to have a test next week and I still can't remember the names of the positions.

"Here. Catch. I'll work some drills with you. That way, the teacher won't give you a hard time." As she throws the ball at me it rolls up my arm and almost catches my chin before I can control it. I feel a twinge along the cut I made last night. A sting bites my arm and my new cut itches. I look up at Chyvonne and she's smiling. Suddenly, it's hard to breathe, as if someone is squeezing my throat shut.

I like Chyvonne. I like the curl of her smile as she handles the basketball. I like her confidence and energy. Her lean frame is built for this game. The height she achieves when jumping makes me check the floor to see if it's hiding a springboard.

But she wouldn't like me. I'm scrawny and definitely not athletic. Besides, I'm a cutter. There's no way she'd be interested in someone like me.

Since I can't keep the conversation going, I watch her throw the ball through the hoop over and over. When Mr. Mackie blows his whistle at the other end of the court, I mistake it for the bell. Without saying anything to Chyvonne, I bolt from the gym. It's not until I'm halfway down the hall that I realize I'm still in my gym clothes.

Chapter 3

Like a Broken Record

On the walk home, TJ, Morgan, and Mandeep follow behind me. Every time I change my pace, they do the same. I live eight blocks from school, but getting home takes forever when I'm the centre of their attention.

"So, guys," sneers TJ, "the new girl — which one of us will be the first to get some of that?"

I can't see his facial expression, but I can hear the tone in his voice, greasy like the pan after Dad cooks bacon.

"You're not asking, you're telling us, right?" says Morgan.

TJ snorts. "You know me too well."

A moment of silence follows. It feels full of danger. Then a hand taps my shoulder — hard — and I realize I've been holding my breath, as I let it out in one hurried rush. "Maybe Travis here thinks he can hook up with her. He was sure eyeballing her on the court. Hell, he was busting out of his shorts."

As I turn to glare at him, TJ laughs and thrusts his crotch forward. Morgan laughs along with him. Mandeep doesn't say anything.

"Right, Travis? Admit it — you want to tap that fine black ass." TJ drills his hand into my chest and I stumble backward.

Eyes up, I tell myself. I try to keep my head from looking at the ground, but I end up looking at TJ's chest instead. *Breathe.* The sudden rush of oxygen gives me enough courage to speak. "*You're the ass.* And her name is Chyvonne. If you try anything on her,

I'll . . ." I lose my train of thought as I think about what they might do to her.

"Dudes, we're keeping the guys waiting," sighs Mandeep. "I thought you wanted to play some more before our game tomorrow." He bounces the basketball he's carrying and nods in the direction of the park.

Morgan turns away from me, shaking his head, and follows Mandeep. TJ puts his fists up and punches the air in front of me. I flinch as he runs to catch up with his buddies.

A few girls from my school are standing close by on the sidewalk. I turn away from their stares.

Dragging my feet, I walk the last few blocks to my house. I look over my shoulder several times, in case the guys change their mind. But I am alone. I stumble up the steps to my front door. Through the basement window I can see Mom running on her old treadmill. I *will* her to look up. I wait for her to smile at me or to wave hello. Her headphones bounce up and down, in rhythm with her jogging. But her gaze remains fixed on some faraway point ahead of her.

Inside, I wander into the kitchen and grab a carton of juice from the fridge. I swallow three gulps, holding the door open. Some leftover steak is wrapped in plastic on a plate. I pull it out, cover it with a lid, and put it in the microwave. Out the back window, I can see our small yard where a crow cackles from the branch of a fir tree. A breeze rocks the branch.

When the microwave beeps, I pull out the sizzling steak, using my shirt sleeve so I don't burn my hand. I grab a bag of dill pickle chips on my way past the counter. Then I head out the back door to the deck.

Other than the crow, it's quiet. But the scene with TJ is fresh in my mind and my chest pounds again as I think of what happened on the walk home. I punch at the air. One, two, three . . . wham! That would be my fist connecting with TJ's face. Then a jab at his stomach — whump! *Shit! Ow!* I punch too low and my knuckles graze the table. As I rub them, I remember the first time TJ and Morgan came after me.

It was during PE and I was twelve. My sisters had just left. Even though they didn't attend my school, they always knew when I had a bad day. So they would have picked up on all the crap in PE. They would have been there to help me out.

I was even punier back then and that seemed to give the guys permission to slam me into the lockers in the change room. They went on about how useless I was at sports. They harassed me about my no-name shoes and pulled at the T-shirt that used to belong to my sisters. We were never rich before the twins went away, but with the cost of sending them to McGill, there's no money left over for sport camps. And even though we don't shop at the Sally Ann, I can't afford name-brand clothes.

But, why target *me*? There were other guys in the class who were short. There were other guys with ripped shirts or baggy shorts that looked like older brothers could have handed them down. I wasn't the only guy who sucked at sports. So, what was it about me that said "make my life hell"?

The first time TJ and Morgan became *physical* with their bullying, I remember shuffling home with a sore shoulder. Morgan had punched me three or four times. I don't remember why, but I do know . . . I didn't hit back. I lay on my bed and punched the pillows, over and over again. When I looked at my fists, curled into balls of anger I could see my veins bulge blue. My eyes traced their intricate patterns along my arm. I could see the blood beneath the surface beckoning to me, inviting me to cut. So I did.

Suddenly, a chill comes over me. It's mid-October and it's cool on the back deck. The sun has dropped behind the fence and it's almost dark. As I take a bite of my now cold steak, I think about Chyvonne. She talked to me in PE, and she wanted to make sure I didn't get in trouble with Mr. Mackie. She didn't say a word about my cheap clothes or the fact that I'm not a star athlete. I think about her golden eyes and wonder what they see when they look at me.

Today wasn't a complete write-off. Today I met someone cool.

On my way into the house, a sickly squeal erupts from the tree behind me as the resident owl chomps on his dinner.

Chapter 4

Brave New World

This morning, I am exhausted. I woke up every few hours last night. Meeting Chyvonne has thrown my world into chaos.

I lean on my arm to keep myself propped up as I fiddle with my cereal and manage to get some into me before heading to school. The air is cool and it keeps me from throwing up the little bit of breakfast I ate. No PE, but that means a double block of English instead. Being this tired, I'll be lucky to stay awake.

I slide into the seat closest to the door. I sit in this spot in all my classes for a quick exit. And it means I don't have someone on both sides of me. My seat is at the front so TJ and Morgan, who sit at the back of the class, leave me alone.

Today there's an empty spot to my left. As a flurry of students rush to their seats, I feel someone standing beside me. I look up to see Chyvonne.

"Are you going to bolt if I sit next to you?"

"Ah, no, I mean, yeah," I answer.

"I can always sit over there," she whispers and points to where TJ has just flopped into a seat. I start to sputter something about TJ being a jerk. But then I see her lips curve into a grin.

Chyvonne doesn't wait for an answer but plops down in the seat next to mine.

Suddenly, a rush of pink and purple hurries into the room and stands at the front of the class. Snickers erupt from my classmates.

The substitute teacher has multi-coloured hair filled with small clips that match the colour of her dress. She pushes her black glasses up her nose and rests her large body against Mr. Follows's desk.

I sneak a look sideways, where Chyvonne is busy rummaging through her knapsack. As she takes out a notebook and pen, she looks up at the teacher and smiles. Then Chyvonne leans toward me and says, "By the way, thanks for sticking up for me." She points to the girls who saw TJ and Morgan doing their routine on me. "Those girls say you defended my honour."

I'm about to tell her I didn't do anything, when the substitute teacher begins to talk.

"Hello students. My name is Madame Belleau and I will be teaching your English class for the next three weeks."

"*Three weeks?*" chime several students together. "But, what happened to Mr. Follows?" asks Sean.

"Apparently, he broke his leg *and* hurt his

back while skiing at Whistler."

Groans fill the room.

"I'm not sure why I was called in for this *particular* job," she says as she walks between our desks. "Not that I'm displeased to have regular work for three weeks, but I specialize in *Art* and *French*. After looking at Mr. Follows's notes, I may be able to add a few flavours to our class that will spice it up a bit."

More groans from my classmates.

"Let's begin with a video," she continues. "Since your unit is a novel study, I want to start with something to get you interested. It's about a *different* way of telling a story."

Several students chatter while Madame Belleau gets organized. Mandeep has to help her with the digital projector. A TED Talk video becomes visible on the screen at the front of the class. She pauses the video. "Before you see the images, I want you to hear Béatrice Coron talk about the 'stories' she has *cut from paper*." She pushes play. A woman walks onto the stage dressed in a coat made entirely of paper. What grabs my attention are the patterns she's made by cutting.

The artist says the story is always there, on the canvas of paper. All she does is cut away the parts that aren't necessary, so the story emerges. I love the clean openings in her art; the lines she makes. It's like the snowflakes we used to fold and cut in elementary school, but on a much larger scale. And they are way more intricate.

As the images flash across the screen, my fingers tingle with sensation — like they want to create something that cool.

The whole class has disappeared. Even Chyvonne. I'm mesmerized by the way this artist cuts paper. When a picture called *Dead City* comes up onscreen, I stand so I can focus on the small details. My chair falls back and clanks to the floor. I realize that everyone is looking at me.

Madame Belleau walks back to Mr. Follows's desk and pulls a sheet off it. After scanning it she says, "Travis, is that your name?"

TJ and Morgan make suggestions like "loser" and "dipshit."

I ignore them and nod.

"Do you have a question?" She returns to the projection screen and zooms in on the image.

It's like she's put a spotlight on me. I fumble for words. "I just . . . I mean . . . I think her work is radical. And brilliant." I grab my chair to sit back down, my eyes glued to the image on the screen. The detail is astounding. Everything is so precise.

Madame Belleau clicks on the next image, then leaves the classroom. I'm still gazing at the screen as she wheels in the cart of computers and says, "Travis, will you help pass these out to students in groups of two. Everyone, pair up with the person next to you."

Groans and sighs fill the room again as people push their desks and chairs together.

Why did I stand up and make a fool of myself? Now, I'm the *one* name she remembers. She'll probably call on me for *everything*.

As I walk to the back of the class, a stack of computers in my arms, TJ puts his foot out and I nearly trip. I recover and finish handing out the computers, then I realize there is only one left. Chyvonne and I will have to share.

Chapter 5

The Dead Are Alive

I smell a hint of cocoa as Chyvonne slides her desk closer to mine. It feels like my heart stretches, like it's waking up. She opens the computer and pushes the start button. As we wait for the home page to load, Chyvonne bites her nails. I have to force myself not to grab her hand to stop her. She catches me watching.

"I know, my hands are a mess. Basketball is hard on the manicure," she says, raising an eyebrow.

Looking at her hands, I want to touch them. Are they as soft as they look? Her lips look soft, too. I feel my body responding to the idea of kissing her, and have to drop my eyes to think about something else.

"Travis, did you hear me?" Chyvonne types in Béatrice Coron and the artist's home page comes up on the screen. I see that most of the students are clicking through the images.

"Sorry . . . something about getting a manicure?"

Chyvonne bursts into laughter. "No. I asked if you want to take the notes, or do you want me to write things down as we work?"

"Oh. Yeah. Sure."

She laughs again. "Looks like you're really into this art?" She clicks on an image called *Dead Building* and without thinking I grab her hand. It's as warm and soft as I thought it would be.

"Stop. Wait. I want to get a closer look at this one. Can I?" I ask, as I move the computer toward me. I type the artist's name and the words *Dead Building* into the search engine. Up comes a better JPEG and I am able to enlarge it.

"She's really good," says Chyvonne. "It's cool how by cutting away parts of the black cardboard, she leaves carvings of skeletons. There are — how many" — she counts — "fifteen rooms in the building? In each one, there's a different scene."

"Yeah," I answer. But I haven't really heard what she's saying. I am lost in the cut-out picture. The artist slices, and a story emerges. Dead skeletons dance in one room. In another they play cards. The *dead* are *alive*.

Chyvonne continues, "I can see setting and character. Not sure I can follow the plot yet. But the picture is definitely telling us a story."

"You're right," says Madame Belleau. I jump. I didn't realize she was by our desks. "I'm really glad you like this work, Travis. And what is your name?"

"Chyvonne. I'm not on your list. I just moved here this week."

"Well, welcome to our school. When we begin the discussion, I hope you'll both share your ideas?"

I cringe. No way am I going to speak up and give the class more to harass me with. I still can't stop looking at the pictures. One of the bottom images shows something that almost looks like bullying.

"Can we check out some of her other stuff?" asks Chyvonne, as she writes down the words: plot, setting, and character.

"Sure. Just one more look." I scan the rooms again. A few of them show one skeleton, alone. My eyes are drawn to a family picture, the only one. A mom and dad are getting a baby out of its crib, or putting it in the crib. Either way, my thoughts crash back to reality.

The image reminds me of the school counsellor I saw a few times when I was in Grade Six. One of my teachers was concerned that I had no friends. She told the counsellor that I seemed depressed. I don't remember what the counsellor and I discussed, only that it didn't help much. I didn't leave the sessions and suddenly start making friends. The bullying didn't stop because I was in counselling, and my mom didn't rush to the door when I got home from school, asking how my day went.

But, seeing the baby in the crib, I remember something the counsellor asked me every session: "Do you feel connected to your family?" I don't remember how I answered for my sisters and Dad — probably "yes." But, for the question about how I feel toward my mom . . . "Numb. Nothing. Nada."

"And how do you think your Mom feels about you?" The counsellor's question still burns clearly in my mind.

"*She doesn't,*" was my answer.

She went on to ask if I had any pleasant memories of my mom. I didn't lie when I said

I couldn't remember one good memory.

I don't know if my being invisible started when I was a baby. But I know exactly how long I've known what to do about it. For the last three years, nearly every time Mom ignored me, I knew where to find relief. I would slice my arm to find balance and to remain sane.

I feel a tug on my shirt sleeve. I look up and Chyvonne is staring at me.

"Where did you go, just now? It's like you weren't even here. Madame Belleau asked you to share what you learned and you didn't answer her."

"Oh. Sorry. Guess I zoned. What am I supposed to say?"

"Forget it," sighs Chyvonne. "I answered for you." She closes the computer and gets up to replace it on the cart. "But since it's clear you are totally into this art, your answer would have been better." She almost floats across the floor. On the way back to her desk, her left hand bounces an imaginary ball.

Sounds like I am still not making a good impression. And that trip down memory lane isn't helping. I can't think of what to say to make it up to Chyvonne, so I pack my books and wait for the bell.

After school, the walk home is quiet. The guys are playing basketball, and I think bitterly that Chyvonne probably stayed to watch. I kick at the leaves littering the sidewalk and take my time. The longer I take, the less time I have to deal with my parents and their empty stares.

As I enter the house, I hear the shuffle of feet and a door slamming upstairs. I call out a tentative "hello." But there is no response.

It sounds like it came from my room!

Chapter 6

Waking the Zombie

I rush up the stairs to find my door partially opened. I can't remember if I left it that way this morning. There is no reason for my mom to go in there. What would she be doing in my room?

I look at the door to my parents' bedroom. It's closed, as usual, but there is a shadow where the door doesn't quite meet the floor. Is that my mom lurking just on the other side of it?

I storm back to my room, slamming the

door and locking it behind me. I rush to my bed and slide my hand between the mattresses. My shoulders relax. The blade is there. But my relief is quickly replaced with being pissed that Mom's going into my room when I'm not home. She has no right to my private world, not if she won't bother with me when I'm right in front of her.

I feel a burn in my brain and my temples pulse. I want to barge into her room and shout at her. I want to tell her how much it hurts. But then I feel my grip on the bed slip. The walls blur. I breathe deeply to keep from passing out.

I realize I haven't eaten since breakfast. My lunch is still in my knapsack. After English class, instead of eating, I went straight to the library to check out more of Béatrice Coron's art. I don't feel like eating now. I just feel lost.

But I know how to find my rhythm.

I pull out my blade. My hand's not steady, so the incision is deeper than usual.

Blood drips onto my clothes. Shit. If Mom is snooping around my room, I definitely don't want her to find clothes with blood on them.

The peace I usually feel after slicing my skin disappears.

Not fair! This is my zone. She's not allowed to infiltrate.

I unzip my jeans and pull them down so I can see my inner thigh. I roll the side of the blade back and forth along the skin there. The hairs on my arm stand up and I shiver. I've never cut twice at one time, but I need to feel that rush of adrenaline. I want to experience the calm that comes when I watch the blood seep away from my body. And my leg is a whole new canvas. It will be like the first time.

I start to make an incision. A small trickle of blood drips down my thigh. Instead of relief, the red seems too bright, too stark.

Béatrice Coron's art is black and white. It doesn't need red to spark off the page!

I nick my leg. *Shit!*

Frustrated, I shove the razor blade back into its hollow in the mattress and stand up.

Zipping my pants, I march over to the mirror. I crash onto my desk chair, my legs straddling it, and stare at my reflection. I try to see what it is about me that causes my parents to shut me out.

I have my mom's long chin and her stringy hair. I'm not athletic like her, but I am slim. If I had my Dad's broad shoulders, I bet I wouldn't be bullied as much. My hair is flat against my head, not like Dad's thick, curly mop. I run my fingers along the light fuzz under my nose, thinking that my dad could easily grow a mustache and beard, if he wanted.

Along with my sisters leaving, a lot of my problems began when my voice started to change, when my body stretched and my face lengthened. Is that what pissed them off? Were they shocked that I was growing up to look like my mom, with no hint of my dad? Every parent wants to see themself in their kids. My

Dad would have to look damn hard to see a trace of himself in me.

Yes, that's when things got bizarre with my family.

That's when I became invisible.

That's when my blade and I became best pals.

Like a caged animal, I pace back and forth. I have to wait until Mom goes downstairs before I figure out how to get the blood stain out of my shirt. I'm still rattled about her being in my room. I wish I had the guts to confront her. But if I open that valve, my mouth is going to spew things I won't be able to take back.

After fifteen minutes of my feet carving the same path in my bedroom carpet, I decide to do homework. Because I'm kind of a freak about school, it's the one thing that makes the days bearable. Besides, maybe it will help my thoughts stay in one place.

I have to finish my math and study for the

test in PE. As I pull out my binder, a note slips to the floor. It's from Chyvonne. Her letters are tight and bold, not flowery like most girls'. She says I missed the assignment. We have to work on a story for any one of the images we looked at on the artist's web page. *Together*. And it's due in two days. Her phone number is at the bottom of the page.

My fingers shake while I dial Chyvonne's number. It rings a few times and then she answers.

"Hello?"

"Hi. Sorry I missed the whole homework thing. We should have worked on it after school." I pause as I try to figure out what to say next. My heart's beating like I've run a marathon.

"Is that you, Travis?"

"Oh . . . yeah."

"I decided to chill after school, anyway. I watched the boys' team play basketball. They lost by a ton. There were lots of botched plays."

There's a pause on the line. I don't know if she's still mad at me for zoning out in class, but to smooth things over I keep the conversation on basketball. "Yeah. I don't usually take in the games. But, I'd watch you play. I mean . . ."

"I'd do anything to play. I really miss my team back home. And what's the sense in taking extra classes if I can't play basketball, anyway?"

"Yeah, I was wondering about that. Why are you taking extra classes?"

"My parents are pressuring me to get into the best university. To do that, I need to have a strong academic program with awesome grades. I do want to play basketball; I just don't know about all this other stuff."

I think about how Chyvonne's all about getting good grades, like me.

She continues talking. "Mom and Dad call me their 'golden girl.' It's like they already have spaces cleared on the mantel for my Olympic medals." Another pause. "They stress too much about my future. They're always on me about something. I wish they'd let me breathe."

Here I *want* time with my parents while Chyvonne has too much attention from hers. "Sorry to hear they're on your case. And it sucks that you don't get to play basketball. Too bad there isn't room on the guys' team. Then maybe they'd win some games."

"Thanks. I definitely would have played today's game differently. They screwed up so many times I was cringing in the stands. But, listen, why don't we talk more while we work on our project? I can't mess up on my first assignment at this new school. My place or yours?"

I think about meeting her parents. If they're over-involved like she says they are, they'll want to meet me. They'll see me for the loser I am, and probably ban Chyvonne from being anywhere near me. My place would be better. Besides, what if a girl did come over? Maybe it would shock my mom out of zombie-mode. I begin to chuckle.

"What's so funny?" Chyvonne asks.

"Ah . . . actually, I was just thinking of how great it would be to watch you rack up the score while TJ and Morgan stand in awe. How about coming over here? I have a laptop computer and lots of space in my room."

Chapter 7

Skeletons or Earthquakes?

Once off the phone, I panic. A girl is coming over to my house, *to my room.*

I scramble to clean up and change clothes. The first shirt I grab has a tear in it. The second one is missing a button but it's clean. As for the bloodied shirt, I hide it under the bed. While I fuss over my hair, my stress increases. Then I tell myself to focus on the homework.

That's something I'm good at.

Once Chyvonne arrives, we look at the

images on my computer. I want to write our story on the *Dead City* art piece, from 2004. She wants to write on *Ayiti Cheri*. It's a picture Béatrice Coron did in 2010 as a fundraiser for Haiti after the earthquake ravaged the country.

"So, should we toss a coin?" I ask with a wink.

"I'm pretty good at coin tosses. We do that all the time when playing basketball. Are you sure you want to take me on?"

We laugh.

"I really connect with this one," I say, in defense of the skeletons.

"And can you communicate with the dead, too?" Chyvonne grins so widely that a dimple appears in each of her cheeks.

"Sometimes I wish I could," I say and then I get serious. I think about why I like this piece. "I guess the picture I want to use is about the dead being dead — being skeletons and all that. I like how they come alive through Béatrice Coron's art. But, I see how yours is more positive; a story about survival and heroes."

Chyvonne scrolls down to the art inspired by Haiti. The picture is cool. An arm rises up from the broken ground where the earthquake has left giant holes. The arm seems to reach for the sky. It's as if the person has been buried under all the rubble and is now surfacing. The images along the arm are of people carrying the injured and finding their families. The way Coron carved the picture, nine neat lines angle up the arm, with scenes in each cut-out.

It seems eerily familiar to me. Each cut along the arm tells a story.

"This is the one I want to write about." Chyvonne rests her gaze on me. "My grandparents live in Haiti and the 2010 earthquake destroyed their home. They both survived, but this picture makes me think of all the people who didn't. It was a scary time." She stares at the picture again. "When I learned we were moving to Vancouver, my parents said it's a city that could have a big earthquake at any time. That scared me. I know it won't happen tomorrow but, hell, you guys have earthquake drills at school."

"I don't think it will happen the day after tomorrow, either. I've lived here all my life and we've never had any big concerns. There have been small rumbles and things might shake in your house, especially if you live on the West Coast of Vancouver Island or Haida Gwaii, but we're pretty good here. Maybe one day I can take you downtown and show you the earthquake-proof buildings."

She relaxes her body at my comment and as she tells me that would be cool, I wonder what I was thinking? I just invited her to *go out with me*. That's not my style. This is already the longest conversation I've had with a girl. Good thing I said *one day*!

She turns back to the computer and leans her head sideways as she takes in the art scene created by Coron.

I put my hand over hers. "Let's go with yours."

As we discuss what to write about first, I hear Mom's voice outside my room.

"Naomi? Dee? Girls, is that you?" Mom turns the handle, but I've locked the door.

"No, I'm doing homework with a friend."

Chyvonne sits on the edge of my bed and shrugs her shoulders. "I'd like to meet your Mom," she says.

I sigh and cross the room. As I open the door, Mom practically falls into my bedroom.

She blinks several times before saying anything. "Well, hello! It's so nice to meet you. I'm Mrs. Elliot. And you are?"

"*Busy doing homework*," I say. I move between my mom and Chyvonne. Mom plows through me to get to Chyvonne.

"I thought my daughters were home. It is *so* nice to hear a girl's voice. It is *so* nice to see you here." Her face lights up.

"I'm Chyvonne." She puts her hand out to

shake my mom's. "Where are your daughters?"

As Mom answers, I move beside
Chyvonne. If she's going to get my mom's
attention, I want some, too. But it's like Mom
is wearing blinders and can only see Chyvonne.

"They're in Montreal, at school. I really
miss them."

"I miss my friends in Toronto. We just
moved here. How old are your sisters?" she
turns and asks me.

Mom doesn't take her eyes off Chyvonne.

"Let's talk about them later," I say. "If we
don't finish this project tonight, we're going
to have to work on it tomorrow. I'd rather use
that time to edit, you know?" I nod my head in
the direction of the computer.

"Good point," she answers. "Nice meeting
you, Mrs. Elliot."

Mom watches Chyvonne walk back to my
desk. I shuffle in between her and Chyvonne.
As I move into Mom's gaze, it snaps to the
ground. She turns to leave, then peers around

my body to my desk. I don't know if she can see Chyvonne, but she quietly says, "Nice meeting you, too. Come by again."

As my door shuts, I rub my arm. If Chyvonne weren't here right now, I know what I'd be doing. But, as I look at Chyvonne, I also see the image on the computer of the arm rising up out of the ground, reaching out.

Chyvonne breaks the silence. "Not to be rude or anything, but that was kind of weird. It's like your mom didn't know you were in the room. I mean, I'm happy she likes me, but doesn't it bother you that she gave all her attention to me?"

I want to walk over to the desk and give Chyvonne a hug. Instead, I shrug my shoulders and nod.

Chapter 8

Clues from the Past

I wish I could act on my feelings. But I'd probably scare the hell out of Chyvonne and she'd bolt. We have to do this work and the more she hangs around, the better I feel. Just past Chyvonne I can see Béatrice Coron's art. In the black rubble that represents the shaken and torn ground of Haiti, eyes peer out from the darkness. It's like they're watching me, waiting to see what I'll do next.

Chyvonne gets that my mom is distant,

but can I *really* talk to her about what's going on? Will she understand?

"It's like . . . I want to . . ." I say out loud, and then plop down on my bed. It's hard to make the words come. Chyvonne perches beside me. That makes it easier to continue. "I'm just happy you 'get it.' That it's not all in my head. Seriously, my mom is like that *all the time*."

"I wish my mom and dad would leave me alone. Not be constantly on my case about practising, and getting ready for the next 'big game.' It's like their whole lives revolve around basketball and me. But now that I've seen what it's like to be . . ." she pauses.

"Ignored," I supply the word.

"Yeah. I guess it's not so bad having my parents be over-involved. I'm really sorry, Travis." She blinks, as if she caught something in her eye.

"I didn't mind it so much when my twin sisters still lived here. The house felt full when they were around. And there was never a dull moment at the supper table. They talk enough for quintuplets. But since they've been gone, it's been really tough."

She moves one leg farther up onto the bed and turns her body so she's facing me. She nods her head.

I keep talking. "My mom does nothing but jog all day. I swear, she's running away from something. I just wish I knew what it was. She's been like this since I can remember."

"What about your dad? Does he pay attention to you?"

"He used to. When the girls were here. He'd talk with all of us. But lately, he doesn't look at me, either. That's why I . . ." I stop myself. I bend my head down so Chyvonne can't see my face.

"That's why . . . what? Go on," she says.

I want to tell her. I want a friend. But I know this isn't the kind of thing you tell people. Especially ones you hope will stick around. "That's why . . . we should get back to our work," I say.

She respects my silence and returns to the desk. She begins typing on the computer. I stand behind her and look at the screen. As Chyvonne flips back and forth between the Word document and the picture of Haiti, I feel an urge to rest my hands on her shoulders so I can feel connected to what she's doing, to her. Her orange sweater sits just off the side of one shoulder, complementing her smooth, dark skin. I imagine what it would feel like to hug her — to hold my body close to hers. But then she might feel *my* skin, the rough marks along my arms. She might feel the dangerous truths etched into my flesh.

I back away, putting physical distance between us.

"What do you think of this?" she says after a few moments.

As she reads the opening lines of the story she's typed, I can only think of one thing. Could

I erase the cuts on my arm? Would tattoos cover them?

Yeah, like I'm a tattoo kind of guy. I tug at my shirt sleeve. Chyvonne takes my hand and pulls me closer.

"Hey, I get that there is something going on. If you want to talk about it, I'll listen. If not, I'm okay with that, too. But we really need to get our story done. I think we make a good team and can nail this if we keep at it."

I agree. Though it's tough, I push my troubling thoughts away and sit down beside her.

I'm impressed with what she's written. "Wow — this is good stuff," I say. I read her words aloud to feel the full impact of them:

It's January and cold on the West Coast of Canada. Night falls early. But day brings sunshine. Three thousand five hundred miles away in a southern island city, it is night for more than a day. It is black in the deep of the morning. And it will be like this for some time to come. Out of the broken earth, a hand rises. Eyes peer from the dirt and crevices. Some can move, some can't. Some will be saved. Some won't.

I've never had trouble focusing on schoolwork. With Chyvonne in the room, I'm distracted. But this art has a powerful message. The despair people felt in Haiti is something that makes sense to me, something that relates to my world. And like the picture, for the first time, I want a different ending.

After Chyvonne leaves I think about how my mom was so excited to see her. I think about Chyvonne's questions and how they were like the counsellor's questions. Does my *dad* pay attention to me? Some of my cuts are from the times my dad cancelled a father-son camping trip, or a day of fishing. He'd plan things then bail on me. Some of the scars on my skin represent the hurt I felt inside.

Then I remember the box in my closet — the box that holds secrets. It's hidden behind my Grandpa's old suitcase. But I never look at it. It's been so long since I even thought about it that I don't recall what's in the box. Did Mom find it when she was in my room? Did she see what's inside?

I toss a few old runners out of the way, then tug at the big suitcase and heave it into my room. I pull out the box and blow on the blue lid to get rid of the dust. A daddy-long-legs walks over my foot back to the darkness of the closet.

The first items I pull out are some old toys. Two matchbox cars and Star Wars Lego: Luke Skywalker and Darth Vader. I've left them here for years, their lightsabers drawn and aimed at one another.

Under the toys are some old school papers with As scrawled across the top. Maybe the glue that has held me together all these years was positive attention from teachers?

And the main thing that holds me together now is my cutting. My first blades, rolled in plastic, sit on top of the papers.

I dig deeper to find some old family photos, pictures from years ago. I look like I might be seven or eight in a few of them. I have the same pale, lanky hair; the same slight build as I do now.

I pick up two pieces of an old photo where I must have cut around each family member years ago. I walk back to my bed and lay them on the cover. They look like paper dolls stuck together. My dad, my sisters, and I look happy. I must have glued us back together standing close to one another. The happy smiles and the collection of items I've just found bring a memory to the surface — a time when my dad sat with me on the floor building Lego.

Maybe he doesn't mean to pull away? He's always busy with work. It costs a fortune to keep the twins at McGill. That might be all it is — by suppertime, he's spent, and has no energy left for talking.

I look at the other cut-out on my bed. Mom stands alone, since I've separated her from the rest of the family. I pick up the picture. Even then, she was wearing grey. But she doesn't look as hollow as she does now.

Things must have gotten worse when my sisters left. How Mom acted today shows how much she misses them. Maybe they kept her grounded, connected. Maybe they helped her get through each day, like cutting helps me. But why does *she* need help to face every day? Why is it so hard for her?

Chapter 9

Drowning

At breakfast, Dad has his head buried in the newspaper again. Mom is in her pajamas and housecoat, shuffling around the kitchen. As I chomp on a hunk of toast, I decide it's time to start figuring out what is wrong with this family. To see if I can put some ideas together.

But where do I start?

"Dad . . . will you always have to work extra shifts?"

The newspaper he's holding muffles his

answer. "Probably. Well, at least until your sisters finish school."

"It's just . . ." I start to say. It's just what? *I want time with you* — can I say that? I take another bite of toast. The peanut butter is dry and some sticks in my throat. I cough. As I walk around Mom to get a glass of water, I try to look into her eyes. I'm searching for a clue, something to help me make sense of my world.

I don't know if she thinks my glance means something else, but she veers away. She makes a wider gap between us as I make my way back to the table. My dad senses the physical and emotional shift in my mom. He jumps up and pulls out her chair. He tries to give her a hug but it becomes an awkward half-hug, before she plops down in her seat.

Dad turns and glares up at me.

"What? I didn't do anything." I put my hands up in the air as I stand by the table.

He shakes his head.

"Will you tell me what I did?" As my voice

rises, Mom shrivels into her seat. Dad whispers some soothing remark that I can't fully make out. It's like he thinks I caused her pain.

"What the hell?!" I shout. In two strides I'm at the garbage cupboard, which I open to toss in the last bit of my toast. I shove my plate in the dishwasher and storm into the hallway. I haven't made my lunch but I don't want another scene, so I head up to my room to gather my books for school.

There's a clanking of dishes, then footsteps coming up to the landing. I hold my breath. The footsteps fade into my parents' bathroom and then I hear the shower running. Since Dad is already dressed for work, it's Mom taking a shower. I grab my jacket and jump down the stairs two at a time. As I turn the handle on the front door, Dad appears from the kitchen. "What you asked at breakfast. I wish I didn't have to work such long hours. Then I could spend more time with you and your mom."

"You mean more time with Mom."

"Travis, I don't mean to . . . It's just . . . I wish . . ."

He doesn't finish his thoughts. I wait, hoping he'll help me make sense of everything. But he picks up his briefcase and begins to head to the door.

"Hold on . . . I'm not done." The words come fast and rough. "I need more answers. Like, why doesn't Mom work? That would take a load off you." And maybe she'd get out more; make friends, and remember how to be a parent.

Again a non-answer from Dad: "She doesn't work because . . . she can't work."

I shake my head. This conversation is going nowhere!

"I'm going to be late for work," says my Dad, looking at his cell phone. "Let's talk when I get home."

"Right, because we *always* talk when you're home."

"Travis, I don't understand why you're asking all these questions *now*."

I hesitate. "I don't know. Maybe because I think . . . maybe it would be good if . . . we could hang out once in a while."

Another awkward silence. I feel my shoulders slump. Dad drops his briefcase to the floor — like he's going to stay and talk to me. Instead, he lowers his eyes from my gaze. He says my name twice, then sighs and reaches for his briefcase again. He turns toward the door.

I give up. Talking never gets me anywhere. I retreat to the kitchen to make my lunch for school. I slam cupboards and shove the drawers shut after grabbing the things I need.

I hear Dad's car pull out of the driveway. The shower is still running. I throw together a ham sandwich and grab two boxes of apple juice from the fridge. If I had money, I'd buy lunch at the school cafeteria. Today is Wednesday. It's always lasagna on Wednesday. Wouldn't that be a nice change from boring sandwiches?

Before I leave for school, I put my foot on

the stairway to the second floor. I think about cutting. The endorphin release would get me through the day. But I hear the running water stop. I don't need Mom being in the same space as me right now.

I can wait until later.

I grab my coat and throw my knapsack over my shoulder, heading out the door. My feet fly out from under me as I slip on the frost-crusted porch. I land on my ass. I groan, knowing it's going to leave a bruise.

On the way to school I try to figure out what got my dad so riled up at breakfast. It's like he's blaming me for something. I just don't know what it is I'm supposed to be blamed for.

Several women with towels under their arms are leaving the rec centre as I pass by. Dad and I used to come to this pool when I was four or five years old. I think it was my first time taking swimming lessons. All the kids in the pool had their moms with them. I was the only person who came with his dad. Not only was it awkward for me, but I think my dad felt strange, too. The other moms didn't look too comfortable with him around, especially since the swimming program was called "Moms and Tots." Some of the older kids doing competitive swimming laughed and made dumb comments.

I remember complaining to my dad after my first time in the pool that I had swallowed too much chlorinated water and felt sick to my stomach. I didn't finish the lesson. The next time we went, I complained that the water was too cold. So, I spent most of the time shivering on the sidelines, wrapped in my towel. I think he tried every trick to get me into the water. But I didn't budge.

Then, the third time, I stayed in the change room, refusing to put my suit on. Dad might have tried taking me a few more times, but I know he stopped at some point. I'm still not keen on swimming.

Now that I think of it, Dad tried to make

those lessons work. He reached out when Mom wasn't there for me. And I ruined the whole thing. It wasn't on purpose, but my actions prevented us from going back to the pool. Maybe Dad *would* have taken me to other things, other events, if I hadn't spoiled it that one time. Maybe some of this *is* my fault?

But, then I remind myself: Mom started that whole scenario by not taking me in the first place.

Only part of it's on me.

Today I tried to reach out; to connect with my parents, and neither one of them could throw me a life preserver.

Chapter 10

Go for It!

Chyvonne and I meet before the bell. We grab a table in the library to work on our story. I can't wait for English class. I really think we have something good here. I tell Chyvonne I came up with more story points last night and she lights up with excitement. That helps put the crappy scene with my folks behind me.

"This is awesome, Travis," she says, as she looks over my work. "You have really creative ideas." Two girls pass our table and snicker.

"Ignore them," says Chyvonne when she sees my expression change.

"Like it's that easy. How come you're so calm all the time? Don't things rattle you?"

"Yeah," she answers, as she copies my new sentences into the story. "I'm rattled by my parents. I get stressed before a big game. I'm worried about my future in basketball if I can't even play. But classmates glaring and whispering — that's about *them*, not me."

"What do you mean?"

"Well, if they have nothing better to do than talk about me, that's kind of sad. And it usually means they don't feel great about themselves — this is their way to get some esteem. I don't need that crap. I guess that's why I usually have guys for friends. It's just easier. No drama!"

"You *usually* have guys for friends?" I tug at my shirt collar — it feels tight. Now I wish I hadn't thought of Chyvonne as more than a friend. *Not interested* — I bet that's what she's trying to say. I just wish I'd figured that out before these feelings started.

"How about this?" She adds a few lines.

Instead of commenting on her next lines for the story, the words blurt out. "But, guys are different. They don't gossip and stare to be mean. They lift fists and connect with people's faces."

"My guy friends and I usually spend time talking *sports*. We aren't like best buddies, we just have lots in common. Drive, and maybe a need to win."

I fiddle with my sleeves. "But with guys it's punch first; ask questions later. Only I've never gotten to the 'ask questions stage'."

She laughs. "I'm not making fun of you, Travis," she says when she sees my face, "just the way you put things. But I believe, even when guys are bullying and pushing others around, it's still about them."

I'm no closer to figuring out the bullying I've faced for years. If it is about TJ and the guys, how come they picked *me* as their esteem-booster? Even talking about it doesn't help me feel any better. I just feel stuck.

Clearly, Chyvonne and I don't have sports or guy friendships in common. But, if we're going to get any work done, I have to focus on what we *do* have in common — getting good grades.

"This is awesome," I say. "In case we don't finish in class, we should meet up after school. Final edits and all that?"

"We could. But, it will have to be after the practice. I've decided to follow up on your suggestion." She smiles at my confused look. "You know. You said I could teach the guys some moves. *I* need a team. *They* need a leader. Maybe it was meant to be?"

"You mean you *are* going to try out for the guy's team?"

"Yeah. What?" She looks at me sideways. "Did you change your mind? Don't think the coach will go for it?"

"No. It's brilliant. It's just . . ." I gather up my schoolwork as I talk. "I guess I don't want anything to go wrong."

"Travis, sometimes you have to take risks. Yeah, they could reject me; turn me down. But that's a chance I am willing to take. How will I know if I *could* have made the team if I don't just go for it?"

She has so much confidence. I wish there were some magic pill I could take that could make me feel that good about myself.

Then maybe Chyvonne would look at me as more than a friend.

But I need a friend. So, I'll do what it takes. "Okay, I guess I can come watch the practice. Cheer you on . . . I mean, if you'd like?"

"That would be cool," she says as the bell rings. We turn in opposite directions to head to our classes.

As I walk down the hall, I realize today is a dreaded PE day. And I just agreed to spend more time at a basketball practice, watching guys who hate me. Thankfully, Chyvonne and I have English before lunch. I'll be in a class I *can* handle with my new friend and ally.

I wade through Science class, anticipating the bell. As soon as it rings, I fly down the hall to English. There, Chyvonne and I continue to work on our story. It's really coming together. But to be sure we get a good grade, we decide to meet after the practice.

Chapter 11

Cutting Blades

At the end of English class, Madame Belleau asks me to stay behind. She tugs at her yellow pants and pulls her long olive sweater up to make it easier to sit on the edge of the table. I stand by my desk as we talk. Her hair is streaked with green today, matching the huge tree that is knitted into her top.

Madame Belleau praises the work Chyvonne and I have done so far, and then gets to the point. "I'm happy you are enjoying this activity, Travis. Seems like the artist really speaks to you. I wish I were teaching art here, but the next best thing is to work with budding artists. Whose classes are you in for art this semester?"

"*Art?* Ah, none. We only get one elective per session and I didn't pick art. I'm not an artist." Even as I say the words, I think of my cuts and how I pride myself on their perfection.

"Sorry." She pauses and looks out the window. "It's just that you were so engrossed in the artist's pictures I figured you were one yourself."

"I love the pictures. I didn't know anyone did this kind of art before. Are there others that do paper cutting?"

"It's an ancient art form, dating back to the sixth century, where it started in China. And now it's popular again. If you have time, I can show you?" Madame Belleau moves to the computer.

"Okay," I say as I hear people talking in the halls. It's lunch time but I don't mind staying to chat with Madame Belleau. She seems genuinely interested in helping me out.

"Chinese paper cutting was a part of the ceremonies to honour spring. The art might picture flowers or animals. Calvin Nicholls is a Canadian fellow who does amazing work, representing animals." She has opened a Pinterest page on her laptop. It's connected to the projector, so the pictures come up on the screen. My jaw drops.

This Calvin Nicholls guy is amazing. It's hard to believe his work is done with paper. The detail on a chimpanzee holding its baby blows my mind. Every hair is defined, each strand, a cut piece of paper. "How does he do this?" I ask, staring. "It looks so intricate. Wouldn't he tear the paper?"

"This art takes incredible patience, Travis. You have to concentrate and make careful moves with your tools. It helps to have a picture in mind or even, perhaps, to have tracing paper you can draw your image onto first. Then you can lay that over your page so you know exactly where to cut.

"Here's another example," she continues. She pulls up a page by an artist named Elod Beregszaszi. His art is folded and three-dimensional. One looks like crazy stairs going nowhere. It pops off the page and demands to be noticed. I shake my head. How can someone do this with just a piece of paper or card stock?

"Here's another Canadian you might appreciate." A new picture bursts onto the screen. "This lady, Myriam Dion, uses newspapers and magazines to work with," says Madame Belleau. "She likes to keep the theme of the *story* present in her work. She sometimes leaves words or pictures intact, in the background, to give more meaning to the art."

As she scrolls down, a house appears. It

looks like an old mansion from a horror story. The inside of the house spills out and flees like crazy thoughts. The terror, the nightmares, and the screams fly out the windows, released for the entire world to see. As Madame Belleau scrolls farther down the picture, I notice a man's head. Why did the artist leave him in the picture . . . outside of the house? Who is he?

"Maybe I've gotten ahead of myself, Travis, but I was excited by your enthusiasm. I brought along some paper of various weights. A scalpel or craft knife usually works best, but a small blade is good, too. What do you think you'll use for cutting?"

Suddenly the room sways. "What did you say?"

"Oh, I just wondered what kind of tool you'd use to do your art? You know, to cut."

I think of my secret spot in the mattress and the sharp edge of the razor blade. How neatly it cuts a line. I wonder what Madame Belleau would think of me using my flesh instead of paper. My arms burn under my shirt sleeves.

"I have to go," I sputter. "Thanks for your ideas." I rush from the room, hearing her voice trail after me, saying that she has supplies anytime I'm interested.

I grab my lunch from my locker. I head down the back stairs that lead to the janitor's room and the school basement, where it's quiet and away from other students. I bite into my ham sandwich. I shouldn't have left like that. Madame Belleau was just trying to help. Now I'll have to apologize. What do I say? *I lost it when you talked about blades and cutting. It all hit a bit too close to home.*

I fold my arms across my chest. I find it soothing to rub my hands along the marks. My cuts — *they* are my art. They are my story. Why would I want to switch to paper? The *feeling* I get when I cut — could creating art give me the same feeling? Somehow, I doubt it.

There are so many days when I've run

home from school to find relief in my blade. If I cover my cuts, will I forget my pain? I *earned* every cut. I am the one who suffered every taunt, every punch. And I found the courage and strength to withstand the pain — to live inside it — to make it my own. I feel tense again, my breath shallow.

Who would I be without the pain — without evidence that I lived every moment?

I realize that the picture I saw today could be my house — it holds secrets, too. If I created art representing my home, it would look like that one. Except for the man. He's not my dad, so why does he fascinate me?

After school, I find a spot at the back of the bleachers to watch Chyvonne practise. During PE she told Mr. Mackie of her intentions, and rather than laugh at her, he seemed interested in her request. Maybe he's tired of his team losing.

I wave when Chyvonne glances my way, and she smiles. Morgan and TJ follow her gaze and give me a look that suggests I should run home now if I want to live. Earlier, they harassed me in gym class. The whole Chyvonne "thing" seems to have them going after me more than usual. I feel myself shrink into the seat. Now I'm wishing I could be anywhere but here.

"Okay, so Chyvonne would like to try out for our team . . . *There are no spots open on the girls' team*," Mr. Mackie says in response to the groans that fill the gym. "I want you to treat her like any one of us. I'd also like to give her a shot at point guard. That's the position she wants to play."

Point guard is TJ's position and I can see worry lines etch his face. Chyvonne keeps her head up. I bite my lower lip and hope the practice goes well. I know how important this is to her. Funny how I'm not the one on the court but I feel giant-sized moths climbing up my throat.

Chapter 12

Beat Down

Chyvonne gathers the group into a huddle and suggests a play. Out of her range of vision, I see TJ and Morgan give each other a signal. I try to get her attention to warn her, but she's already started the game. They move down the court. One of the team members passes the ball to Morgan and he deliberately misses it. I look at Mr. Mackie and wait for him to whistle down the play, but he lets it go.

On the next play, TJ grabs the ball.

Chyvonne is open, but he doesn't pass to her. He waits for Morgan to get close and then throws the basketball when it's clear there is no way his teammate can get it. The other team grabs the ball and scores at the opposite end.

Chyvonne puts her hands on her hips and mumbles something I can't hear.

Then Morgan says, "Guess you don't really know how to call them, hey? Wants to play friggin' point guard . . ."

"Watch your tongue," says Mr. Mackie. Even though Morgan isn't tossed from the game, Mr. Mackie calling him out for teasing seems to piss TJ off even more. As the players switch off the bench, except for Chyvonne, TJ leans in to talk with Morgan. Chyvonne gathers the next set of players in a huddle.

This time the play goes well. Mandeep gives her a high five after he sinks the basketball in the hoop.

"Now, that's more like it!" Mr. Mackie shouts. He shakes his head at the bench, where

Morgan and TJ are sitting. They look up at me as Chyvonne smiles in my direction.

For the next couple of plays, things go well. Chyvonne's calls go as planned and I get caught up in the game. I become so engrossed in the play on the court, that I don't see TJ climb the bleachers until he is standing in front of me.

"So, you're here to support your *girlfriend*? What I'd like to know is how a loser like you scored a piece of action like her. If she's into white guys, why the hell did she pick you? She must be an idiot."

Without thinking, I fire back, "Yeah, well her plays on the court are pretty smart. Too bad she doesn't have a team that knows how to follow them. But then . . ." I point to the court as Mandeep sinks another basket. "I guess *he* has it figured out." Mr. Mackie claps and several players whistle.

TJ shoves my shoulder so hard I fall back into the crevice between the seats, where I am totally vulnerable. That seems to be all TJ needs. His fists are perfectly in line with my face. I can't move fast enough. He swings his right arm and his clenched hand clips me on the chin. My jaw shakes. My teeth rattle. It feels like my brain loosens inside my skull.

I scramble to move. He blocks me.

"Here's something for her to *figure out*," TJ's voice is filled with contempt. "Tell her to find her own team and leave *my* position alone. Then maybe I'll let you live."

"Maybe if you knew how to play the game —" I start. Before I can get my bearings, TJ punches me again. This time his left hand makes contact. He just misses my nose. Close call. It would have broken for sure. I feel a tooth fall loose and catch it with my tongue to keep from swallowing it. I'm in a tight jam and I can't shift my body to stand up.

TJ sneers and his fists make contact again, and again. I lose track of how many punches he throws. As I try to breathe, blood catches in my throat and I roll over coughing. My tooth flies out and lands in my open hand.

Between breaths, I hear Mr. Mackie call for TJ and his line to get ready for their turn on the court.

My body is crumpled between the seats as TJ hops back down the bleachers, rubbing his left hand as he goes. I don't want anyone to know what's happened, especially Chyvonne. When I look down to the court, she's laughing with Mandeep.

These few minutes have been hell for me, and she's playing "best pals" with the enemy!

My heart blasts against my chest wall, as I jump to the ground from my spot on the bleachers. It's too high. My ankle twists as I land. My foot throbs with pain.

I look back to the court. Chyvonne hasn't noticed my fall. Instead, she has her arm around Mandeep's shoulder. She fires off instructions for the next play. He taps her on the back as they split up and take their positions on the floor.

As I pass the garbage can I toss in my tooth and watch it land on a chocolate bar wrapper. I roll my tongue into the new empty space in my mouth and taste iron as I swallow blood. Limping, I head out the side door of the gym, which leads right into the staff parking lot. Madame Belleau practically knocks me down as we cross paths.

"Sorry, Travis! I didn't know there was a door there. Oh my gosh, are you okay?"

I put my hand up to my face. As I pull my hand away, I see blood. Madame Belleau fusses in her purse and produces a tissue.

"Here, use this," she suggests. I wipe away the blood and continue to stare at the ground. "What happened, Travis? Should we get the principal?"

"No, I'm cool. I just need to get home. I have a bit of a headache."

"Well, you should be careful. You might have a concussion."

"No. Honestly, I'm good. I just want to

get the hell out of here." I begin walking away from the cars. Madame Belleau puts her arm out and gently holds my shoulder.

"Travis." Her voice softens. "I can see something is troubling you. If you ever want to talk, I'll listen." She tilts her head. "Can I share something that always helps me? Get lost in a piece of art. Let your talent take you to a place where *you* control the outcomes. For artists, art is what nourishes the soul."

She rummages in her bag. "Here. These are the papers I told you about. You might find something useful. "Oh," she puts her keys in the door of an orange Volkswagen Bug. "And you'll need a rubber mat so your blade doesn't get dull. I don't have any right now but if I get a chance this weekend, I'll pick one up for you at the Art Store in White Rock."

I take the papers from her. She opens her car door. "Do you need a ride home? I'm not sure I'm allowed to drive students, but you look distraught. Are you sure you're okay?"

"I can get home," I say, and add, "Thanks." I watch her back her car out of the space in the parking lot, and then I make a beeline across the field.

I can't wait to get to my blade.

Chapter 13

The Fallen Heart

As I head for home, rain drips from the clouds like snot from a runny nose. The drops get bigger and I don't have a coat. Along with my knapsack, it is still in my locker at school. No way in hell am I going back now.

The papers from Madame Belleau are getting wet. I stop under a cedar tree for some cover from the storm and roll them, so at least the inner ones will be protected. I can't cover up my body and my thin shirt is getting soaked. A nasty chill climbs inside my bones and my torso shakes.

As I cross Thrift Avenue, a car rips around the corner and water spews up in a wave. "Asshole!" I yell as the driver continues on down the street. I'm drowning on the sidewalk. My jaw hurts. Chyvonne's face flashes into my mind, but it doesn't comfort me. I see her smile light up the gym — the smile she's giving to Mandeep.

I can hardly lift my legs to climb the steps to the front door. I don't look to see if my mom is downstairs. I throw off my wet running shoes and trudge up the steps to my room. Once I close the door, I pull out the stack of papers from Madame Belleau. The inner ones are dry. I unfold them and lay them on my desk. I spread the wet papers out on the carpet, where maybe they'll dry.

When I sit on the edge of my bed it's as if all my old feelings are right there. Like they were tangled up in my sheets, waiting for me.

Flashes of Chyvonne and TJ cut at my flesh, as though I've already pulled out my blade.

For a moment, I think of calling the twins. But there's a three-hour time difference between Montreal and BC — they'll probably be out partying. Could I tell my dad what's been going on? Fear and shame grab my bones and hold me paralyzed on the bed. So I pull out my blade.

I slide it back and forth. The razor's smooth surface is like ice, like glass. It's like something dangerous, but beautiful at the same time. As I roll up my sleeve, I see the black construction paper from Madame Belleau that I laid on my desk.

I think of the art I saw on the Internet.

I think of this afternoon and TJ.

The blade rolls along my arm. I don't cut; I just feel the cool sensation against my flesh.

I can see the bleachers. The neat rows of seats and steps, lines that meet at right angles. Open spaces between them. It's the spaces that are dangerous, where you are most vulnerable.

I look at the paper again. It appears to rise up. It's as though it turns on its side, so I can see how to make the bleachers. It seems to show me how to cut it so those lines exist, so the seats are visible. I push the blade and it barely pierces my skin.

I think of Calvin Nicholls and how his attention to detail makes his art bigger than its own canvas. And like the pop-up art of Elod Beregszaszi, my vision is three-dimensional. I see the entire scene. But how do I create this image?

My heart pumps furiously against my chest. The pounding rhythm matches the movement of my blade. My eyes focus on the paper again. I see how easy it would be to cut the black, to hack at it until my heart is exposed. I could show it split open, revealing how it's nothing but a cracked organ, a damaged piece of myself, bare for everyone to see. Especially Chyvonne. How it tumbles down the stairs . . .

Blood trickles onto the bed cover, but I ignore it as I envision the last step. The rectangular shape that waits for my heart to stop falling, for it to crash-land, exposed and helpless. I jump, and the blade pierces my skin, as I imagine a foot — TJ's foot, waiting to crush it.

I slide the blade to catch the small stream of blood that slips down my arm. But the red doesn't grab me. Instead, this burning ache in my head, this image I've created in my mind, wants to be released. It needs to be realized.

I seize the black paper and grab a slab of wood I used to use for jigsaw puzzles from under my bed. I place the paper on top of the wood and watch as the blade hits the paper and cuts. It slices. It cuts some more. The first few hits are good, but then I cut too fast and the paper rips. My breath is hurried and heavy. My eyesight is blurry.

I grab a thicker piece of paper and begin to cut again. It's as though I don't see paper or picture. All I see are figures and motion, a sense of what I want the final image to be. Each cut gets me closer to that realization. Something alive fills my veins and energizes me.

It's like a drug and I want more.

As pieces of black paper fall to the floor, steps appear, then a heart. As more paper shards fall away from the canvas, the picture emerges. The heart rolls down the steps, splitting as it goes. A foot is raised just above it, at the bottom stair.

After what seems like hours, I finally lean back against my bed, spent.

I've cut an entire scene. What I imagined is now real, with rich detail and a visible story. Having it on paper puts the pain *outside* of me, like I've been released from its hold. I feel lighter than I've ever felt before — even lighter than I feel after cutting my flesh.

I feel exhilarated, like I'm drunk. I begin to laugh, thinking how I should thank Mr. Follows for breaking his leg. How else would I have learned about this kind of art? How else would I have discovered that something inside me could feel this good?

My creation sits on the slab of wood on the floor. My head hurts and my heart feels tired.

I can still see Chyvonne on the court with Mandeep. I let myself be vulnerable and that opened the door for TJ to crush me. The only person listening is a substitute teacher, and she'll be gone in a few weeks. But at least she's helped open a new way for me to see things — introduced me to a world that matches mine, and expands it.

As I think back over the last few years, I realize that without some of my past teachers, I wouldn't have made it this far. But then sometimes having their attention and knowing they cared about me, made it harder at home. If they showed affection toward me it made the gap between my mom and me seem that much wider. So their good intentions drove me to my blade more often.

Today my blade landed on a new surface. I cut my pain into black paper instead of pink flesh. And it kept the grey from overwhelming me.

Chapter 14

Treadmill

The doorbell rings. I move to my bedroom door and press my ear against it. I don't hear a thing, so I unlock it and crack it open, just a little.

I can hear Mom schmoozing with Chyvonne. Her voice sounds sickly sweet and her tone says she'd replace me with Chyvonne in an instant. Then there are footsteps on the stairs. As I rush to my bed to hide my blade, I forget to lock my door. It whips open before I can put away the picture I've made.

Chyvonne enters the room.

As I scramble to pull my sleeves down and try to kick the picture under the bed at the same time, I can see it's too late. Chyvonne is already taking in the scene in front of her. She looks first at the paper slices littering the floor. Then I follow her gaze to the drops of blood beside the picture. After glancing at my art, she rests her eyes on me.

"I can explain," I sputter. "See, I cut myself while trying to make this picture." I pick it up and throw it onto the bed. "I'm still trying to figure out how to do this stuff."

"Picture? Forget the picture! What the hell happened to your face?"

I involuntarily move my hand to my cheek. My tongue seeks out the hole where my tooth had been. "Oh yeah, I forgot. It's nothing, really."

"*Really*." Sarcasm and worry taint her voice. "You call this *nothing*?" She takes my shoulder and turns me so I can see myself in the mirror. My nose is red and bulging like the noses of those old guys who booze too much. Even though TJ missed my eye, the dark line of a bruise is forming under it. I look disheveled. But maybe part of that is from my frenzy in creating art?

I turn from the mirror and sit on my bed. Chyvonne puts her hands over mine.

"What the hell, Travis? Who did this to you?"

I ignore her concern. "It doesn't matter." I pull my hands away. "What I'd like to know is how you and Mandeep made out?" I can hear the snarl in my voice.

"What? What are you talking about?"

I move to the door and close it. I think I can hear my mom's feet creaking on the stairs and I don't want her listening in. "Looked to me like the two of you were the only ones on the basketball court. Maybe if you hadn't been so cozy with Mandeep you'd have noticed what was going on in the bleachers."

"Seriously?! What did you think I was doing? Setting up a date?" Her tone notches up a decibel.

"Keep it down. My mom . . ." I gesture to the hallway with my head.

Chyvonne lowers her voice. "I thought you were happy for me. Supporting me." She shakes her head. The imaginary basketball flips back and forth between her hands. "When I'm in a game, I don't see anything but the court, the ball, the players, and the hoop. I definitely don't see what's happening in the bleachers. I can't afford to — it could cost me a play. It could cost me the game."

"Well, it almost cost me my life," I say. I know that's an exaggeration, but I don't care. I want her to feel guilty. I want her to feel as bad as I do.

Her face turns red. She lowers her head. Now, I feel like a shit for wanting her to hurt. And I finally know what she means when she talks about playing basketball. While cutting the picture, cutting my art, I zoned. I stopped watching my bedroom door. I wouldn't have heard her coming in.

I see the picture on my bed: my heart, the foot poised above, ready to crush it. I thought the foot was TJ's. But now I see it could just as easily be Chyvonne's. "You need to leave," I hear myself say. I move back to the door and hold it open for her.

"What?"

"Go . . . just go."

"But . . ." I hear the sound of my mom's feet shuffling down the stairs. As I close the door I hear Mom asking Chyvonne what's wrong. I don't catch Chyvonne's response as the front door clicks open and shut.

I jump to the window and stand off to the side so Chyvonne won't see me. But, as I pull back the curtain, she is looking up. I step back and then slide down the wall, suddenly exhausted.

The heating vent is under my butt. It leads

down all three levels to the basement, where my mom has retreated now that Chyvonne is gone. I hear the treadmill start up. The whirring sounds of the turning belt rise through the vent.

I bend my head closer and I'm sure I can hear Mom's breathing get heavier as she runs. I bet she wishes she could run straight to Montreal and the twins. I bet she wishes she could run away from me.

Somehow, *I'm* the trigger for *her* pain.

I cut nearly every time she's around — *she's* the trigger for *my* pain.

I sit up and can still hear the whirring and breathing. I can hear the whirring thoughts in my head, my breath and Mom's breath.

My head is heavy and I lower my chin.

Chapter 15

Timing Is Everything

When I wake up, it's dark outside. The lamp on my desk has been turned on and is shining a small circle of light. My dad is sitting on the edge of my bed with my paper-cut art in his hands.

"Dad, what are you doing in here?" I stand too fast and have to lean against the wall for support. My throat's dry and I'm thirsty. There's a rumble in my stomach.

Once I get my balance, I shuffle over to

the bed. My digital clock flashes 10:04.

"This is really good, Travis," Dad says. He holds the paper up and the light passes through it, reflecting the cut-out image onto the wall. The heart tumbles down the stairs. "Looks like you had a tough day?"

"Oh, this," I grab the picture from him and lay it across my bed. "This isn't me. It's a copy of some work we saw at school today."

"I didn't know you were taking art. Your grandma on your mom's side was a wonderful painter. Did you know that?"

"No. Yeah. Maybe." *Why is he in my room? Why is he suddenly so interested?* "Dad, what do you want?"

"I was concerned. You skipped supper. Your mother told me you had a fight with your girlfriend and I wanted to see if I could help."

"Oh, *the fatherly talk*. Right, I've been waiting for this." I walk to my desk and move my papers around. I want Dad out of my room, but I can't think of a reason to get him to leave. He finally wants to connect and all I can think of is how to get rid of him.

He pats the bed beside him. I remain standing by my desk.

"I want you to know, Travis, it's not only that I understand what it's like to have girl troubles *at your age*. I mean, I'm going through the same thing *right now*. It's been hard for your mother and me. All I could think of while I watched you sleep was how I let you down. How I haven't been the best role model for dealing with relationships. This shouldn't have happened."

"What shouldn't have happened?" I ask, not following his train of thought.

"I guess your girlfriend was quite concerned about you and asked your mom to check on you. Your mom passed it on to me. I can see why you didn't come to dinner. You were hoping I wouldn't notice that you'd been in a fight?"

I snort. "If you can call it that. I didn't

get one punch in. No retaliation — just humiliation. And for the record, Dad, she isn't my girlfriend." I look at my image in the mirror and now see my face the way Dad must see it. The way Chyvonne must have seen it. I'd be freaked out, too. But all I can think to say is, "Too bad Mom didn't come to check on me herself." I walk toward the window and look out on the bleak night. Everything is shrouded in heavy black and it's hard to make out the house across the street.

"Travis, you know your mom loves you. She's just not very good at showing it."

"The first part is a lie."

He doesn't answer but stands up and joins me at the window. His voice softens. "She's worried about you, even if she can't show it."

I wonder if someone can worry about you without loving you?

I don't feel hungry, but I suddenly know a way to get a few moments to myself, to think and to clear my head. "Dad, maybe some food would be a good idea. I can't remember when I ate last."

"Right. I'll get you something and bring it upstairs. I don't think your mom should see you like this."

As the stairs creak from his weight I sit back on my bed. Mom *should* see me like this. What I look like *outside* now mirrors my feelings *inside*. And these feelings aren't just from today.

It's weird how, in the picture, first TJ, and then Chyvonne trampled on my heart. Now, I can't help but think how my mom has hurt it. Before, things upset me and I cut — scars formed on my arms to match my feelings. This time, the hurt was carved into a picture.

When I cut my flesh, I don't think of who hurt me, or why they caused me grief. I focus on the sensation in my body. But with this art, it's easy to see how I've been hurt by more than one person. And how one person has hurt me more than any others. Even though

I'm bummed out by everything that happened today, creating this art helps me understand the impact people have on me, especially how their actions affect me.

I lean the picture against my wall. It's pretty good. I feel a cool sensation travel through my veins, just thinking about creating this art. I could easily become addicted to *this* feeling. But what if I never have another artistic vision? What if this is the only piece of art I ever create?

The door pushes open and Dad enters with a sandwich and glass of milk. "I hope this is okay?"

Suddenly famished, I grab the first sandwich half and eat it in three bites. Dad picks up the remote, turns on my TV, and props up the pillows on my bed. He plops down and motions for me to join him. "Isn't this one of your favourite shows?" he asks.

I choke on my next bite, but bring the plate and glass to my bedside table. I hesitantly slip in beside my Dad. But I tell myself it's only because I'm sore from sitting on the floor. I'm cold and I'm tired. As I settle my teeth into the sandwich, Dad bursts out laughing at something on the screen. I don't pay attention to the show or my food. I just wonder what happened today and how the hell I ended up here.

Chapter 16

Meatloaf and Mashed Potatoes

School is not high on my list of priorities today. I try to fake the flu but Dad sees through my lie. He tells me I look much better than I did yesterday and that I should confront my nemesis. Funny thing is, I don't know which one he means.

I find some of my sisters' old makeup in the bathroom and apply it to the bruises on my face. It doesn't do much to cover them, but I figure everyone is going to know anyway, as TJ probably lit up social media bragging about it.

I purposely wait until after the bell to go to class. English is first block and I'll do anything to avoid talking to Chyvonne. She's in her seat but I don't look her way as I sit down. She slides an envelope onto my desk. I pick it up and turn it in my hands. Do I really want to open this now?

Curiosity wins — I rip open the flap and pull out the blue paper tucked inside.

I know sorry doesn't cut it, but that's what I feel. I didn't know what was happening in the bleachers, but if I did, I would have stopped the play and come to help you. I wouldn't have been so smug for kicking TJ's butt on the court. But, I wanted to ham it up with Mandeep, because I knew that would piss the guys off, and I figured you'd enjoy the show. How was I to know what was going on outside of my range of vision? Here I thought I was making you happy. And I was feeling good doing what I love to do best, playing basketball. I am sick that you were hurt and I couldn't help. And I'm sorry I didn't know what to say or do at your house.

Chyvonne

P.S.
Just for the record . . . I do like you.

My cheeks burn at the last line. I feel as if I've just stuck my head in a pizza oven. I glance sideways at Chyvonne. She's smiling but that only makes it worse. She leans over and is about to say something when Madame Belleau asks us to be the first to do our presentation. I completely forgot it was due today.

Great, now I have to stand up in front of my peers with a mangled face that's overheated with embarrassment.

This time, I can't bolt. As we walk to the front of the class, I tug at my shirt sleeves to be sure they cover my arms. Snickers arise, as some of the guys catch sight of my face. A few girls look upset and try to focus on Chyvonne instead of me, but mostly my classmates just stare.

Chyvonne and I haven't decided who will read what, but Chyvonne takes a breath and recites the first few lines. When she pauses, I know that means it's my turn to read. We continue on like this until the story is done, sharing the reading load. Several times I hear my classmates gasp or say "hmm" — they are engaged in the story we are telling. I hadn't noticed, but now I see that Mandeep is in charge of the computer and has projected *Ayiti Cheri* onto the screen.

When we finish, the class breaks into wild clapping. Madame Belleau says, "bravo" repeatedly, and Chyvonne grins from ear to ear. For once I'm not being ridiculed. And it feels good to know I didn't let Chyvonne down. Had I stayed home, she would have had to present by herself. A strange feeling courses through my body and I realize this must be what confidence feels like.

As I return to my seat, Mandeep leans over to me and says, "Dude, not like I want to hang out or anything, but what TJ did is crap — he shouldn't have pulled that shit." I feel a smile inside and nod in Mandeep's direction.

While my peers present their stories, I let everything that just happened simmer into my bones. It feels pretty good.

Once the class is over, Chyvonne and I head into the hall together and walk toward our next class.

"Since tomorrow's Friday," says Chyvonne, "I wondered if I could make things up to you by taking you to a movie?"

A new fear grips me. One I don't know how to fix. What will Chyvonne and I have in common now that our assignment is done? And even if we hang out, what happens next?

"I — I can't. My turn to . . ." I stall, trying to think of something that sounds plausible. "My turn . . . to make dinner."

"Sweet. You rotate cooking at your place? What are you making?"

I need another lie. "Meatloaf and mashed potatoes." It's one of the few things I do know how to cook.

"I know it's not cool to invite yourself over, so I won't, but maybe we can hang out after dinner? Go for a walk? You could show me your artwork? Or we could head to the rec centre and I could show you some basketball moves? I know how much you *loooove* the game!" she teases.

I do want her to come over. When TJ and Morgan aren't around, I like being near Chyvonne. Maybe things could get serious between us? But what about my cuts? I could keep my arms covered in the beginning, but not indefinitely. At some point she'd find out, and then what?

Another voice in my head says, *Then I might as well be alone, forever.* That's what's left. I could become a recluse — a starving artist. Starving for attention, that's what I would be. Is that all I have to look forward to? After last night's artistic release, Chyvonne's apology, and today's storytelling, I finally feel connected. I don't want to lose that.

Before I've decided what to do, I hear myself inviting Chyvonne to dinner. "But you can't make fun of my cooking skills. I only got a C+ in Home Ec."

"Done," she laughs and heads in to the room for her next class.

As I sit through Math, all I can think about is tomorrow. Why did I invite Chyvonne to dinner at my house? I don't want a repeat of the last time she was over — Mom hovering and feeding on Chyvonne's presence like a vampire. Dad treating her like she's a trophy I've won. No, I'll catch up with her at lunch and cancel.

Chapter 17

Exposed

When I get to the cafeteria, I see Chyvonne heading for a table. She's got a tray loaded with food: salad, roast beef, noodles, two hard-boiled eggs, and milk.

"I need protein," she says as she notices me staring at her plate. "Coach will let me know in PE if I made the team. If I am the new point guard, then I'll need to be 'on' for the game. They're playing the best team in the league after school."

I sit across from her at one of the cafeteria's skinny tables. They're long enough for about twenty kids but we're the only two there at the moment. Our hands are touching in between bites of food.

"You'll be fantastic," I say.

"I'm a bit nervous. I'm not usually one to stress out, but I have so much riding on this."

"You're in. Trust me."

I bite into my sandwich. It's turkey today, instead of ham. And my carrots have white splotches, showing their age.

"If I make the team . . ."

"*When* you make the team," I say.

"Right. If we win today, then we're off to a tournament right away. We'll be heading to Victoria for the weekend."

Although it means being at the site of my last humiliation, I tell Chyvonne I'll watch the game. "As long as Mandeep follows your plays, you guys will be great! Maybe TJ and Morgan won't be able to make it — wish I could think of some way to keep them out of your hair."

She laughs and her warm hands slide up inside my loose shirt sleeves, pushing them up to my elbows. Before I can pull away, her fingers trace the crevices along my arms. Her eyes focus on the scars — taking in the cuts.

My body freezes. I don't blink.

Her hands and body are motionless. I can't hear her breathing. I can't hear anything but a wild hum in my ears. I don't want to see her expression change. I lower my head. A herd of students from grade twelve crash into the seats around us.

Chyvonne withdraws her hands suddenly like I have a plague.

My secret is exposed — I am exposed.

I stand abruptly, and my hand swipes Chyvonne's open carton of milk. It spills onto one of the guys who just sat down.

"What the hell!" he says.

In seconds, I climb over my seat and push past the students coming into the cafeteria. I bolt from the room. I bolt from the school. I book it home as fast as I can go.

Once I am in my room I slide my hand in between the mattresses. Out comes my blade and I nick my arm before I can even roll my sleeve. Red drops rise from the skin. The red matches my feelings — horror, anger, and embarrassment. I didn't want Chyvonne to discover my cuts. I didn't want her to find out in a public place, where I can't even explain.

But, now I won't get to explain. Her silence told me everything I need to know. In my panicked state, I push the blade into my arm, again. More blood. I'm not cutting my skin — I'm stabbing it. I'm erratic, and confused jabs at my flesh aren't helping. I look at the paper from Madame Belleau. I think of the house — the one with secrets, the one that looks like it's out of a horror story.

I have demons running around inside me. Is that what made Chyvonne pull her hand away so fast? Not the cuts, but what the cuts say about *me*.

I drop the blade to the floor. I grab the wooden slab from under my bed, and place a new piece of black construction paper on it. I jab at the paper instead of my flesh. I cut away the parts I don't need. Paper flies as adrenaline pushes the blade.

First, I make an outline of my arm. Half the page becomes my mottled flesh, filled with cuts. Real cuts. With my blade, I create openings in the paper where you can see right through. On the other half of the page, I cut paper away to make an arm that is softer, smoother. That arm pulls away from my hand. No, it reaches for my hand.

No, it pulls away.

* * *

It's dark outside, so I must have slept. My clock shows 11:45. I should just go to bed, but what happened today is shaking my insides. As I lift the art I crafted out of my pain, I realize my outsides are shaking, too. The paper rattles in my hand. The two arms, no longer intertwined, haunt my thoughts.

It's not the right time to seek help from my family. It's three or four in the morning in Montreal, and Dad has to work tomorrow. But I need some help. Maybe I can find something on the Internet?

I open my laptop. I have an e-mail account but I don't check it. I'm afraid of what it might hold — or not hold. So, instead I type the words *self-harm* and *cutting* into the search bar. Pages and pages come up and, as I scroll, one website grabs my attention. It's a page filled with messages from young people who cut, like me. I read their stories, which are depressing and only make me feel heavier. This isn't what I need.

I return to the search page and open a window that talks about *help* for cutting and self-harm. Lots of information, but something sticks with me right away. One page says cutting is like putting a band-aid on an emotional wound that needs stitches. It doesn't get at the real source of the pain, so the wound rots and decays.

The more I read, the more things begin to make sense.

Another article says that people may cut to be more like their peers who cut, to get status, or acceptance. *That's not me.* I find an article that suggests people might feel more alone after cutting, and there may be a level of shame. *That's me, for sure.* And it says that carrying the secret is a heavy burden.

Now Chyvonne knows, so my burden isn't as heavy. But she recoiled from me. How do I move forward with Chyvonne? Is there any future for us?

I read some more. The next section talks about triggers — been there, done that! Mom, Dad, my peers . . . and my anger — they're my triggers. But it also says that when you are finally ready to talk about it, you have to give the other person time to work through their feelings around what you just shared.

My eyes blur as I read.

I finally hit the sack at about three a.m. but my sleep is restless. I wake up two or three times, feeling as though I've missed something. It's like I failed to catch a plane going somewhere. I see myself running down the tarmac, chasing the jet. A hand reaches down to help me onto the stairs before they fold into belly of the plane. I run faster, stretch my arm to reach out for the hand. Each time, I wake up just as our fingers touch.

Chapter 18

Running from the Truth

Today, I want to stay home. But that would mean being around Mom all day. I couldn't take that — not without any sleep, not with the stress of my "outing" at school. It's just too much to bear.

But maybe there is *one* person I could talk to, who could help. Maybe there is one person who can bring a little balance back to my world.

I head to English class well before the bell.

But I realize I don't want her to think of me other than as an artist. So, I won't share about my cutting.

Madame Belleau is sitting at Mr. Follows's desk.

"Good morning, Travis. I heard the good news. Chyvonne made the boys' basketball team. That is one brave girl! I could never do what she did. But then, I was never great at sports. *Art* saved me." She heads to the blackboard and begins to write down some words. Her hair is orange today. So is her long skirt and sweater.

"Madame Belleau?"

"Yes, Travis?" She turns to me as I speak. Her eyes have the caring look that I never got from my mother.

"I like Chyvonne." I'm not planning what to say, the words just spill out of my mouth. "She's cool and I agree. She's brave. But I think I scared her yesterday."

"What do you mean? What happened?" She puts down the chalk and sits on a student's desk. She waves her hand at the desk beside me so I sit. The halls are empty. On Friday mornings most students arrive late.

"I . . . we . . ." I sigh. How do I say any of this? "We had a fight. Sort of. I walked out on Chyvonne. It helped me to sort through things by making a picture of it. I tried paper cutting a couple of times this week. One is of the school bleachers, and one is two arms . . . reaching for each other."

"Wow! That is fabulous news. I mean, about the art. Not that you and Chyvonne aren't getting along. Do you want to talk about what happened?" She looks sincere and I can tell she'd listen. But she looks a bit uncomfortable at the same time.

"No, I'm good. I just want to talk about paper cutting. I catch the paper a lot. I've torn a few pieces trying to get used to working with the different weights."

"Ah. Yes, it can take time to figure out what works best."

I nod. She goes to Mr. Follows's desk and pulls out a fabric bag. It's full of paint brushes. She carefully pulls out something and returns to sit with me. "I have a blade here that my friend gave to me when I told him one of my students was interested in paper cutting. He suggested you check out the art programs at the Emily Carr Institute down at Granville Island. There are some post-secondary programs there that might interest you. Start thinking about this now, so you can register in art for next semester."

I haven't thought about my future — not at all. I don't think about life after school. I don't know if there is a life after grey.

"Thanks," I say, taking the tool from Madame Belleau. It looks like a pen but with a retractable blade instead of a ballpoint. I slide it into my back pocket. Madame Belleau talks as she finishes printing her message on the board. "I hope you'll show me your art, Travis. Even if you can't bring it to school — maybe you could take a photo?"

The bell rings.

I freeze.

As the students come in, I hear them congratulating Chyvonne on making the boys' basketball team. Turns out she helped them win for the first time this season. A ripple of pride for her success courses through my veins. I want to turn and congratulate her. But I can't bear to see the disappointment in her eyes.

Chyvonne calls my name. Without thinking, my body stands upright. Next thing I know, I'm in the hallway, fleeing from class. I skip the rest of school and end up shuffling through stores in the mall and hanging at the park. My head is full of jumbled thoughts. I spend the day walking aimlessly around town until school ends.

I can't believe that I'm glad we can't afford a cell phone for me. I'd go crazy checking every few seconds to see if Chyvonne has texted me — or even more crazy, if she hasn't. Once I get home, I remember that I was supposed to be making supper tonight. Right! *Like that will be happening.* I can hear Mom downstairs, running on the treadmill. It's not only the way I look that I've inherited from her — running must be a family trait!

I jump the stairs to my room. As I fire up my laptop, the websites I looked at last night are still open in my search feed — the messages about getting help, and what to do when someone wants to offer support.

It says that people may turn away when they first find out. That's what Chyvonne has done. My hands tremble as I scroll down the page. I feel an urge to grab my blade, to add a new mark — a new story. But that would mean avoiding what's really going on inside me. For the first time, I realize I need to experience these feelings.

As I wipe my eyes with my sleeve, the doorbell rings. Mom must not be able to hear the doorbell over the treadmill, as it rings again.

I debate opening my door but then I hear Chyvonne call out, "Hello. Is anyone home? Travis?"

I guess she let herself in because the door handle to my room turns. "Travis, can we talk?"

This is one time I can't run away. I have nowhere to go. My pulse quickens and my body prepares for flight. In a second of panic, I contemplate jumping out my window. But that's not an option.

My legs trudge to the door. My hand turns the lock and Chyvonne swings it open as I retreat to my desk.

"You're not going to bolt? I have a feeling that's your M.O."

"Among others," I say.

She doesn't respond. My room rings with the same silence as in the cafeteria.

Chapter 19

Porcupines and Chameleons

The silence is awkward as I try to think of something to say. I blurt out the only thing that comes to mind: "Congratulations on making the guys' team — and your big win. Bet your parents are proud."

"Yeah, but that's not what I came here to talk about."

I fold my arms.

I didn't expect to ever see Chyvonne here again, so my art is out in the open. Both pictures are sitting on a low table on the other side of my desk. Her eyes move toward the table and then she slides across my room to pick up the bleacher art.

"Look, I have a ton to learn," I say. "It's not that good . . . really."

"All artists say that. I know how stoked you've been about the stuff Madame Belleau has shown us." She holds the picture up and then puts her head down. "Shit, this is about me, isn't it? This is about the whole TJ mess the other day. Is this your heart? I definitely wouldn't trample on it like that, Travis. I am so sorry. Sorry for everything."

"What do you mean by 'everything'?"

"Yesterday. In the cafeteria . . . I'm sorry about that."

"About what?"

"I didn't mean to freeze like that. I was in shock. I didn't know. I was confused. Maybe scared."

"Scared of me?"

"No, scared of . . . you know. What those cuts on your arm mean." She drops onto my bed and sighs. "Travis, I don't know what to say. I don't know how to talk about this."

"I don't either." Chyvonne didn't have to come to my house. She doesn't have to stay in my room. But sitting on my bed suggests she isn't about to leave.

She looks at me. Her eyes are wide and filled with tears. "Tell me what's going on. Why is this happening?"

"You know why."

"I *don't*, Travis. I only have an *idea* of what life must be like living in a house where you're ignored. I only have a *sense* of what it might feel like to get beaten up by jerks who have no status unless they're picking on someone." She reaches across to where I'm sitting at the desk and takes my left hand in hers. She doesn't slide her hand up my sleeve along the cuts. But she is dangerously close.

"I couldn't tell you," I answer. "About

the cuts, I mean. I wanted to — that day we wrote our story. But I convinced myself that *you* would be the one to bolt. I figured you wouldn't accept me if you knew what I'd done. Since you pulled away at the cafeteria, I guess I was right?"

"As usual, you use all that good grey matter of yours to come to the wrong conclusion. I pulled away — yeah. I was surprised. That kind of stuff isn't on my radar. I know it's real. I just didn't know it was real for *you*. I didn't realize your pain ran that deep. Hell, until yesterday, I didn't even know guys actually did stuff like that."

I pull my hand back and hers slips to her side. I begin to stand but my legs are shaking.

"Travis. That's not what I mean. I mean that I didn't know guys could externalize their pain that way. But it makes sense. You feel pain and then add . . . more pain. But I thought you actually had a handle on things. I mean, we talk . . . sort of. You got so much out of the art we've looked at I guess I thought maybe that's how you work things through. This stuff," she points at my two pictures, "it looks like it helps? I just never suspected . . . I was caught off guard, and . . ."

"So you were surprised . . . not disgusted?"

"No, of course not! Worried. Confused. Scared."

"Scared . . . that I'm a freak?"

"No . . ." She takes a deep breath. "Travis, I was quiet in the cafeteria because I was trying to figure out what to say. I didn't want to say the wrong thing and push you away. Drive you to do something worse. I'd never live with myself if that happened." She takes my hand again and pulls me toward the bed so I can sit down beside her.

"Travis. I was trying to figure out if these were cuts that you made yesterday or if they were cuts from a long time ago? I was wondering if you feel this kind of pain *right now*? I guess I was gathering my thoughts.

Then you took off, literally, within seconds of me pulling my hands away. Spilled milk, a jerk giving me a hard time about you — I figured you'd gone to the bathroom. *To get yourself together*. I gave you five minutes. When you didn't come back to the cafeteria, I left to go find you. You were gone."

"I didn't know what else to do . . . I *want* things to be different with us. I *am* dealing with things through my art. But that only just started. You and Madame Belleau — you've made things . . . better. I feel . . ." I can't find the right word.

"I just wanted to be there for you, Travis. You've helped me, too. I was new. Didn't know anybody. No team to play on, and you encouraged me to go for it with the guys' team. I got to help my team get their first win. Now, we have a good shot at making the playoffs."

She continues, "Look, I want to be friends. I want to be . . . more than friends." She leans in and kisses my cheek. "But, one important thing. Shouldn't you tell someone about this? Like the school counsellor, or Madame Belleau?"

"No. Definitely not! I'll get a handle on things."

"Okay. But now *I know* what's happening. Maybe letting *others know*, who can help, will make a difference?"

"What will it matter? You're the only one I care about. That is, if you still want to be around me . . . if *you* don't change your mind and decide to run."

"I'm not going anywhere, Travis — remember, we already established that's *your* M.O. I just think your cuts say something. They show your pain. I mean, really show it. Right there on the surface. Am I right?"

"Yeah."

"Well, I hope I can help you — but I'm no pro. Think about what I said — there are loads of people who can help. Okay?"

"Maybe." I shift uncomfortably. I don't like

this part of the conversation. I stand again but I don't have anywhere to go. Chyvonne stands, too. I don't want her to leave. "Listen, can we let this go, for now?" I ask.

She nods.

"Can I show you something?" Changing the subject helps me ground myself again. I pull up the art pages on my computer so Chyvonne can see them. I open the JPEGs of Calvin Nicholl's first.

"Whoa! These are incredible," says Chyvonne. She seems relieved to focus on something else. "Check this one out," she adds, as she turns the laptop toward me. It's a picture of a porcupine. "I think this is me — if I were to choose a favourite."

"Appropriate choice," I tease. "You *can* be prickly at times!"

Chyvonne laughs and stands like she is going to attack me, but in a playful way. She sits back down and scrolls with the mouse. "Which one would you be, Travis?"

I don't even have to look at the screen. I've studied them so many times in the last few days, I know exactly which one matches me. "The chameleon, what else?"

As we look at 3-D paper art and Myriam Dion's work, I not only feel grounded again, I actually feel inspired. My fingers are itching to create.

"You know, Travis. It's kind of cool."

"What is?" I ask. She reaches over and laces her fingers with mine.

"That you've become so interested in this. It's like your 'thing.' Your passion. I have basketball and you have art."

I think about how cutting is my thing, too. But since the incident in the bleachers, every time I've pulled out a blade, it was to create art on paper. I'm about to say something when Chyvonne continues.

"I hope you know, Travis . . . that what happened at school, it wasn't about me retreating from you. It was more like a moment . . . of reflection. Putting everything in perspective."

"I get that now. I'm good at bolting *and* jumping to the wrong conclusions. I think I have my brain set to some mode that makes me misinterpret things."

"Hey, I'm just glad we sorted things out. And guess what? Madame Belleau returned our paper today and we got an A on our story for English. That will definitely help my grade point average!" She moves toward my door. "Now what about the meatloaf and mashed potatoes you promised me for dinner?"

Chapter 20

Dinner for Four

In the kitchen, I pour us each a glass of iced tea. I rummage through the cupboards and find the ingredients I need for the meatloaf. Luckily, we have ground meat in the freezer and some potatoes that need to be used today or they won't be any good. Chyvonne and I chat while I cook. She pores over my laptop to find the best page for me to study for our basketball test on Monday. Even when she's quiet, I am comforted by her presence. And

I realize she's probably right. I should talk to someone. But, it doesn't have to be right away.

At supper, the table is vibrant with conversation and it feels like my sisters are home. My mom is especially involved and asks Chyvonne hundreds of questions. Chyvonne brings the conversation back to me at every chance she gets. "We just got our mark in English for the project we did together this week. And our grade is awesome. Did Travis tell you what a hit we were?"

"I'm happy to hear that, son," says my dad. "You've always been good at schoolwork. Don't take after me on that one. That's your mom's influence, for sure."

I glance in Mom's direction. She's so focused on Chyvonne, I'm amazed she doesn't swallow her whole, like the old witch I remember from fairy tales as a kid. I don't think she hears my dad. Chyvonne shifts uncomfortably in her chair.

"Chyvonne is taking extra classes at school," I say. "She's the smart one. Going to get a basketball scholarship to a great university. Especially now that she'll be racking up the wins on the guys' team." She smiles at me and her feet seek mine out under the table.

Mom seems impressed, then shares her love of running and how she was a star track team member in school. I'm learning more about Mom during this one dinner talk than she has ever let me see.

"Where do you like to run?" asks Chyvonne. "I have to keep in shape for the game, so I've found this great spot in Huntington Hills Park. Have you ever run there before? It has these great trails that go —"

"Huntington Hills . . . Hunt . . . don't you know? You can't . . . you can't go there . . ." Mom stutters as she shouts, *"EVER AGAIN!"* Standing abruptly, she almost falls, as though she's drunk. She rants some more as her body presses across the table toward Chyvonne.

"Do you hear me, never! That place is seething with creeps just waiting for a sweet girl like you. Don't go there . . . just DON'T." Mom's breathing is erratic.

I don't know what just happened. How did we go from talking like a real family to Mom flipping out and shouting? Panic drives into my bones.

Dad stands and puts his arm around Mom's, guiding her back to her chair. Her eyes are wild and I can see that Chyvonne is frightened, too. I take Chyvonne's hand in mine. Mom begins to sob. Dad moves behind her chair and she leans into his chest. Her body heaves with emotion. She keeps repeating the same words, "Don't go there. Don't go there."

I'm scared by what I see, but embarrassed, too. I look at Chyvonne and motion to the stairs. She places her napkin on the table and follows me out of the kitchen. We hear my dad whispering to my mom as we approach the landing to the second floor. I look down to the kitchen and see from my dad's face that he is just as scared.

"Jesus, I'm really sorry, Chyvonne," I whisper. "I don't know what the hell got into my mom. She drives me crazy, but I didn't think until just now that maybe she *is* crazy."

"That was really weird. I was pissed that you weren't getting any air play in our conversation, but I was happy your mom seemed engaged. Her outburst was out of the blue. What did I say? What did I do wrong?" Chyvonne's hands are shaking.

"It's not you," I reassure her as we enter my room and I close the door. Bits and pieces of the past surface. I remember how my sisters talked about Mom being an athlete. How she used to jog outside. How she used to wear bright pink outfits to exercise in. How she used to teach classes at the local gym. That was before I was born. After I came along, things changed. She never stepped outside to jog again. The basement became her whole world.

Her whole world turned grey.

"I think something about the park spooked my mom." As soon as I say it, I know that I'm on the right track. "A long time ago, I think she used to run there. Maybe something terrible happened to someone and my mom stopped going. You know, afraid it could happen to her, too?"

"Is there a chance something *did* happen to her? Like a mugging, maybe?"

"Haven't a clue. Until now, I haven't thought about the park, or how my sisters say my mom used to be so outgoing. I don't think she was a loner back then."

Chyvonne takes a deep breath and sits on my bed. "When did things change?"

"When I came along. See, I'm the reason the whole world sucks."

She takes my hand as I sit beside her. "But you just said it has something to do with the park. She was fine at dinner until I brought up the name of that stupid park." She bows her head. "I wish I'd never opened my big mouth."

"You couldn't have known. Hell, I didn't know. I'm not even sure my dad knows. I wish my sisters were here so I could ask them what they remember. All I know right now is that whatever happened to make my mom the way she is . . . it all happened before I was born. And now I know that some crazy park is also to blame."

But if it happened before I was born, how am I the problem?

I wish I'd brought my laptop back to my room. We could do a search on Huntington Hills Park around the time I was born. Or I could e-mail my sisters now that I have something concrete to ask them. But my laptop is in the kitchen. It's in the same place where my mom just lost it. I can't face her right now. I'll check it later, when I'm on my own.

I need to get my emotions in check. They're bubbling out of control and I don't want to resort to old patterns. "I hope you got enough to eat. Before my mom flipped out, I mean."

"Yeah — and it was good." Chyvonne seems relieved to focus on something other than the incident with my mom. "You're not a half-bad cook. But you're an excellent artist. I hope you'll show your work to Madame Belleau."

I can tell by the expression on her face that she doesn't want to leave me alone. Maybe she's worried about what I'll do — that I'll turn to my blade?

I am still thinking about my mom. I hope once Chyvonne leaves I will be able to talk with Dad. If he hadn't come into my room last night, I'd feel alone with this. I'd probably be sorting things out the way I usually do, with my blade and my flesh. But the fact that Dad hung out with me makes me hopeful that we can talk. And after what I saw at dinner, we definitely have a ton to sort out in this family.

Chapter 21

The House That Screamed

Dad doesn't come in to talk with me after Chyvonne leaves, but stays with my mom in their room. I can hear them whispering late into the night. In the darkness, I pace for hours.

But I must have fallen asleep because I awaken suddenly, still in my clothes. I'm certain someone is in my bedroom. I turn on my lamp but no one is there. I'm sure I was being watched. I creep over to my door and open it a crack, but there is no one in the hall. Snores are the only sounds coming from my parents' room.

I close my door and let it click shut quietly. Maybe I was dreaming? Somehow I think that, just before waking, my dream was filled with shadows. It was full of things lurking in the dark. I want to create a picture of what I dreamt. I want to put it on paper.

But how do you make shadows visible?

Suddenly it comes to me — the black needs to stay! It will represent the shadows. I have to cut away what isn't in the shadows.

I think about all the paper-cut pictures I have seen in the last few days.

I pull out some paper and the slab of wood. I don't even think about releasing my blade from the hiding spot in my mattress. Instead, I grab the knife Madame Belleau gave me. I push the clip and the blade appears. It's strange, but I don't think once about slicing my skin. Instead, a fever begins to rush through me as I think of creating shadows and what they represent. My dream unfolds itself into cuts on the page. I slice and rip. Shapes take form.

Just like before, the release of adrenaline fuels my work. My hands fly across the page; paper falls to the floor. I sit in the midst of mayhem. Through the window, the clouds break and a bright orange moon provides additional light and shadow on my floor. This drives me on. Nightmares from years ago, and the bizarre happenings at dinner, pass through my fingers and onto the page.

I finally sit back to see what I've done.

I can't actually make sense of it all, but it looks like there are trees strangling other trees. It seems everything in the picture has a nightmare counterpart, a shadow behind it that is larger and more dangerous.

The centre image is of a baby, floating in solitude. The space around it is immense. Nothing touches it.

It's strange how I can almost hear the

baby's cry. The trees around the centre, the ones being strangled by those behind them, all seem to be reaching out to the infant, trying to grasp it.

I don't know exactly what the picture means, but just like my other work, I feel as though I've been purged of something. I suddenly have questions for Mom and Dad, and wish they were awake. I think I might be that baby, lost and alone, in the centre of something that doesn't make sense.

As I place the art under my bed, change into my pajamas, and crawl under the covers, I hear a piercing scream. Mom shouts for help from the next room and then I hear Dad's low voice, comforting her. Suddenly, I remember all the times as a young boy I would awake to my mom's screams. How could I forget how often she had nightmares when I was little? Had she finally tamed her demon, only to have our dinner talk set it loose again to haunt her nights?

Am I the demon?

I hop from my bed, without turning on the light, and pull the picture out again. The moon provides enough light and I see that one figure emerges more clearly than the rest. How did I not notice this, moments ago?

It isn't a tree that I see in the corner of the picture. Instead, I see the outline of a woman and a shadow behind her, more powerful than the others. More like a man, than part of the forest. I can see how if I added a splash of pink, that woman could be my mom. But who is the man behind her?

A panic grips me and I slump to the floor, the picture still in my hands. Out of the corner of my eye, I see the light in my room grow brighter and I realize the door is opening. I sit up and hold my breath. I know my fear is unreasonable, but I can't stop the pounding of my heart. It wants to burst from my chest.

Mom is in the doorway.

"May I come in?" she asks tentatively. I

don't know if I nod or not, but she comes in anyway. She sits on the chair at my desk, far enough away that she is hard to see in the dark.

"I just want you to know . . ." she pauses to take a breath. Her voice gets softer, not louder. I have to strain to hear what she is saying. The shadows play havoc with her image; her eye sockets seem empty. I sense something big coming, and try to quiet my pounding heart. "I just need you to know that . . . none of this . . . none of this is your fault. It was never your fault."

I want to see her face, her expression. I'm about to get to my feet when she steps back. I feel her recoil.

"I'm sorry," is all she says as she stands and rushes out of the room. I slump back against my bed, watching the shadows in the hall. Then I see Mom scramble around my dad to get down the stairs. I hear the front door open and moments later I hear the car race out of the driveway. Mom drives off, still in her pajamas.

Dad stands in the doorway to my room. I'm trying to figure out what the hell just happened. He comes to sit beside me on the floor.

"I don't know how to say this, Travis. I never wanted you to know the truth. I didn't think it could do any good. But I see now that it doesn't matter whether we ever talked about this or not, the incident has always been with us, always waiting, ruining our lives."

"What are you talking about, Dad?" I ask. "Please, tell me."

Dad puts his hand on my knee and begins to cry. His words come in choked waves. "Your mother. She . . . she was the victim of . . . your mother was jogging one day in the park. You are a result of . . . it's because of that *bastard*!" I can't make sense of his words, but they terrify me.

Noticing the picture in my hand, Dad stands abruptly and turns on the bedside lamp. "May I?" he asks, reaching for the picture.

I shrug and hand him my art. He studies it, then says quietly, "You knew? All along you knew what had happened?"

"I don't know what you're talking about, Dad."

"This picture. It's of your mom, isn't it? It depicts the day . . . she was raped."

"*What*?" I try to stand, but my legs buckle and I slide down to the floor again. Acid fear climbs into my throat. I feel nauseated.

But if my mom was raped, if this is the terrible thing that happened before I was born, then I'm . . . I can't finish the thought. It's too horrible. I snatch the picture from my dad and claw at it frantically, the openings widening until there are no more shadows. I tear at it until nothing remains but holes and gaps ripped into the paper.

My dad puts his arms around me. I'm numb again. But in a different way. I don't want to cut to feel something. I am numb because the feelings overwhelm me — I'm *inside* the feelings as they settle into my bones. I let Dad hold me. Let him carry some of the weight of what I just learned.

We stay that way until I can't keep my eyes open.

Epilogue

Beyond Grey

It's been two weeks since Mom lost it at dinner. She and Dad used all their air travel points to book Mom on a flight to Montreal so she can spend time with my sisters. Maybe she'll get better, but I don't know. As they leave to head into Vancouver and the airport, my dad turns to me and says, "Everything will be better, son. I promise." He calls me *son*. Even though I've been wondering what will happen between the two of us, it gives me hope that he has kept those three letters in his vocabulary.

I don't beg for Mom to stay. I am sure that we both need a change and some distance to figure things out as a family. I trust that Dad and I will start to talk more. With only the two of us, we'll have time to work things out as a father and son.

Before I head up the stairs to my room, I look out the window as my parents get into the car. Mom is wearing a pink sweater that my Dad bought for her earlier this week. He waves as the car pulls out of the driveway.

It's November in Vancouver. Usually, we're socked in with rain. But, this morning, although the air looks crisp with frost, the sun is shining. I'm glad I live on the West Coast, where the trees and lawns stay green. Our neighbours have a garden with plants my dad said are zinnias, and they're still blooming with bright orange flowers.

Once the car is out of sight, I climb the stairs to my bedroom. I don't think about what

I'm doing. My body just goes through the motions. I walk toward my bed. My sleeve is rolled. My hand pulls out the blade. I rub it against my cheek. I slide it back and forth until I get a rhythm going.

Then I pull out a piece of red paper and begin to cut.

Acknowledgements

Thank you to my writer's group for your suggestions. Thanks to my parents for helping with edits to the story and for championing a tough subject! And most especially, thanks to my fabulous editor, Kat. I appreciate all your hard work to help make this a better story and for seeing its potential.